Union of the Witch

Crypt Witch cozy paranormal mystery series - book 15

K.E. O'Connor

K.E. O'Connor Books

UNION OF THE WITCH

ISBN: 978-1-915378-13-2

Written by: K.E. O'Connor

Chapter 1

"Keep your head down, or the demon will see us and make a run for it, and I'm not chasing him all over town." I crouched beside my half-sister, Zandra.

We'd been skulking around the shadowy alleyways in Mudacre for three hours, and there was nothing pleasant about this place. It was a strip of gambling dens, cheap bars, and greasy looking takeout joints. Even Wiggles would turn up his nose at the pizza on offer if he was here.

"Paxos isn't going to show." Zandra's scowl looked scarily similar to mine when I realized I'd run out of brownies *and* the cookie tin was empty.

"You don't know that for sure. And this is your chance to learn the business. You can put your magic to good use by bringing down demons as my side-kick."

"Side-kick! You'll be my side-kick if my power keeps growing."

She wasn't wrong. Zandra had a natural ability for the darker shades of magic. And as an untrained witchling, that could mean trouble for anyone who got in her way.

"Besides, I already put my magic to good use." She shuffled along beside me, kicking aside a broken chunk of brick.

"Stop making so much noise. Anyone would think you don't want to find this demon and arrest him."

"Maybe I don't. What's wrong with demons, anyway?"

"Oh, I don't know. They terrorize innocent people, they have a tendency to flay, dismember, and destroy at a moment's notice, and they leave piles of foul-smelling goo everywhere. They also—"

"Yeah, yeah. I get the point. Witches are awesome and demons are bad." Her gaze ran over me.

I adjusted the demon catching bag hanging off my belt loop. "Have you got something on your mind?"

"Well, you know, Frank and all." She gestured at me. "I figured you must have some affinity with demons, since you've been carrying one around for so long. Some of that demon badness must have rubbed off on you along the way."

"Nope. Frank rubs no part of me. And if he ever did, I'd have myself magically deep cleansed. And having an unwanted demon lodger inside me doesn't mean I'm making friends with other demons. Now, focus! What are the five tips I've told you when you're on a demon hunt?"

"Something about pizza and blah, and blah de blah blah. And I forget the rest."

I groaned. Zandra made a terrible student. Not only had she reverted to acting like a fourteen-year-old, she hadn't listened to a word I'd said about how to track a demon and cause the least amount of damage when capturing it.

I wrinkled my nose. We were so similar that it was painful to witness. Had I really been that bad when learning how to perfect the art of demon hunting?

Most likely.

But I wasn't going easy on Zandra. She'd crossed the line recently and misused magic. I had to put a stop to that before it got noticed by the wrong people, or more specifically, the wrong angels, and she got arrested.

"I see something up ahead." Zandra shot out a light ball.

I killed it instantly and grabbed her by her collar. "Stop joking around. We only use spells around non-magicals in an emergency."

"I figured that spotting a demon was an emergency." She struggled out of my grip and stepped away. "Haven't we done enough demon hunting for one night?"

"We don't stop hunting until we find this thing. Paxos put six people in the hospital."

"Six non-magical people in the hospital."

"And your point?"

"They... err... well, wasn't it their fault they got hurt? They got in his way."

"He barreled through a funeral, stole the corpse from the open casket, and punched twenty people. And he set the chapel alight and vomited goo all over the wake buffet. This is a bad demon. He needs stopping."

"Let the angels deal with him. We're out of boring Willow Tree Falls for once. Let's go have fun. We could try out a casino. I know a few spells that guarantee we'd walk away winners."

"What's so boring about our home?"

Zandra kicked at the ground. "It might be your home, but it's not mine."

"Sure it is. You've been there for months. It can be quiet at times, but I like it."

"I only stay around because I haven't had a better offer."

I grabbed Zandra's arm and yanked her behind a huge dumpster. A second later, a huge pile of gray demon goo landed where she'd been standing.

Zandra's eyes were wide with excitement as she stared at the goo. "Let's go grab ourselves a demon."

"Wait! Not so fast. Take a good look at the goo deposit."

"I'm not poking around in demon muck. I don't know which hole that goo came out of."

"Look at it. Demons emit different secretions in a range of colors."

Zandra nudged the lump of goo with her foot. "I'm guessing this is some kind of demon with a bad head cold."

"Gray goo doesn't come out of the demon we're hunting. When Paxos is angry, he spits out a shower of orange goo. Don't get that on your skin or it'll burn."

Zandra glanced up. "We've been tracking the wrong demon all this time?"

"No. I know how to track demons. All this shows is that there are more of them on the loose than we realized. And sometimes, the demons just like to hang out in dark alleyways, make scary noises, and dump muck on people's heads for fun."

"Which is annoying but not exactly terrifying," Zandra said.

"It depends. If you were trying to get to sleep while some creepy thing with claws and a tail tapped on your window and spat goo at you, you'd be terrified."

Zandra shuddered. "Give me nightmares, why don't you?"

"And imagine not being able to defend yourself with magic? That's why we're out here."

"We should just use magic to find him. Throw out a few detection spells, and we can grab ourselves a demon. Maybe we could get them both. Do we get a bonus if we snag more than one demon?"

"Nope. All we'd do was annoy Dazielle if we brought back the wrong demon."

"It doesn't take much to annoy her. She's always snappy."

I nodded. Dazielle had a stressful job heading up Angel Force, but she had been a giant pain over the last few months. I'd been keeping out of her way until she'd offered me a paid gig hunting Paxos.

"How about this? If we catch the demon, we can take the rest of the night off," Zandra said.

I gritted my teeth as I stalked along the alleyway. I'd hoped that bringing Zandra with me on demon hunting missions would give her a positive channel for her magic, maybe even inspire her to become a demon hunter and use that spiky magic she struggled to control for something positive. But she wasn't interested.

"This is boring," Zandra muttered as she caught up with me. "Why drag me out with you to do something so dull? I don't see you bringing Aurora on demon hunting missions."

"There are two problems with having Aurora here." I pointed to my chest. "One is the demon inside me who wants to grab her and make her his plaything. And Aurora's magic is pure. It's about positivity and bringing people joy. Demons don't want joy. They want destruction. They react badly to happiness."

"You're saying my magic isn't pure?"

I arched an eyebrow at Zandra. "You've had your moments since you moved to Willow Tree Falls. You're more a blast first and ask questions later kind of witch."

"And that's a bad thing? It's kept me alive this long."

"It's a bad thing if you attract the attention of Angel Force."

"I can outrun those feathered idiots. Or out-blast them with magic if I have to."

There'd been a time when I'd thought exactly the same thing about the angels. And most of the time, they were still pretty idiotic, but I had a decent bond with some of them, and I'd learned it was never wise to ruffle their feathers. For all their angelic smiles and soft fluffy wings, they packed a powerful magical punch.

"Let's keep looking for our demon," I said.

"Only if you agree we can take a break in half an hour. My feet are aching."

"Sure. If we've not found any signs of Paxos, we'll grab snacks from the least dodgy looking takeout place."

Zandra worried me. She hadn't had the best upbringing, but I was determined to make sure she didn't fly off the rails and get herself in trouble. But sometimes, she skated too close to the dark side of magic, and I wasn't certain I'd be able to catch her if she tipped off track.

Twenty minutes of pointless alleyway searching later, we were still no closer to finding Paxos.

"Let's take that break," I said. "What snacks do you want?"

Zandra grinned and bounded along the alleyway, swinging her arms. "Ice cream."

"It's freezing out here. How about hot chocolate?"

"We could go for hot fudge sundaes? There must be a place around here that's still open. An all-night diner that does dessert. I'll cast a—"

"No! No spells." I checked the time. It was two in the morning. The only places around here that would still be open were dodgy bars and clubs.

I rounded the corner and walked straight into Zandra, who'd stopped dead on the sidewalk.

She grabbed my arm and yanked me back.

"Did you see the demon?" I whispered.

Her eyes were wide as she shook her head. "No, someone much more interesting. Take a look and see for yourself."

I peered around the corner and scanned the quiet street. It took a minute, but then I spotted a figure skulking in the shadows on the opposite side of the road. He was tall, wore black jeans and a leather jacket with the collar turned up. My heart bounced down to my toes and back up into my chest.

"That's Rhett, isn't it? The guy who ditched you for his buddies and left Willow Tree Falls without even saying goodbye," Zandra whispered in my ear.

I winced. That hit too close to home. "That's not exactly what happened." It was exactly what happened. Rhett left after an argument we'd never resolved, and I hadn't seen him since.

"The way I heard it, he showed up for Aurora's fancy wedding and then vanished on you," Zandra said. "He didn't even ask you to dance at the reception. What a jerk."

"He has his moments. Don't we all?" I huffed out a quiet breath as I continued to watch Rhett. *What was he doing here?*

A finger jabbed into my ribs.

"Ouch! Quit doing that." I glared at Zandra.

"It is true, though. He did walk out on you?"

"It's sort of true. It's also complicated." I felt abandoned by Rhett. I hadn't seen him for ages and had almost given up on him.

My treacherous little heart was bumping away like it had just had an electric shock, making me think all kinds of dumb thoughts like running after him or rationalizing that there must have been an emergency for him to leave so suddenly. It would all make sense once he'd explained everything to me, like I was a needy girlfriend with no life of my own.

Rhett hadn't even sent me a message to say goodbye. He'd simply upped and left, leaving our relationship in tatters. I didn't even know if I was single since we hadn't officially ended things. I felt very single, but I couldn't deny the way my heart pounded at seeing him again.

"What do you think he's doing lurking about in a dump like this?" Zandra said.

"I've no idea." I hadn't realized it, but I'd moved out of the alleyway and was standing on the street corner.

"Tempest! Let's follow him," Zandra said. "Don't you want to know what your shady ex-boyfriend has been getting up to? I would if he was mine."

My eyes narrowed. "You're too young to have a serious boyfriend." I couldn't tear my gaze away from Rhett. He was making sure no one paid him any attention as he slid from shadow to shadow, his head down and his gaze on the sidewalk.

"Stop treating me like a kid. I'm only a few years younger than you."

"Which is still young. And dating leads to trouble. My advice is not to do it."

"You mean the kind of trouble you find yourself in by creeping around dark alleyways after your missing boyfriend?"

"Exactly." I took a step in the direction Rhett was walking then stopped. What was I doing? I wasn't the kind of woman who chased after a guy.

"You're desperate to find out what Rhett's up to." Zandra grabbed my arm and hurried me along the sidewalk. "I won't tell anyone we followed him. It'll be our secret."

"It won't be a secret, because that's not what we're doing." Still, I kept walking. It seemed I had treacherous feet and a treacherous heart.

"Isn't he usually with his gang?" Zandra said.

"They're probably around here somewhere."

"Doing something they shouldn't?"

I shrugged. Rhett's biker gang walked a murky gray line when it came to illegal activities. Since he'd taken over the gang leadership, he'd calmed the group, and they mainly stayed on the straight and narrow, but none of them were angels, Rhett included.

Zandra yanked my arm so hard, she almost dislocated it. "Is that his bike?"

I pulled my arm away from her painful grip and rolled my shoulder. "It looks like it."

"I've been testing out a flying spell. I could use it on both of us. We could tail him from the air. He wouldn't know we were after him." She touched her palms together and sparks of magic flew from her fingertips.

I grabbed her hand and squeezed until the magic faded. "No flying spells. No magic of any kind while we're in the open."

Zandra rolled her eyes. "Don't you want to know what he's up to? This would be killing me. I'd have to know."

My gaze lifted as Rhett's bike roared to life and he zoomed away. Of course I wanted to know what he was doing. But I didn't chase after any guy, no matter our history or how gorgeous he was. Rhett had let me down big time, and if he ever crawled back to Willow Tree Falls with his gang, he'd have a lot of making up to do. And even then, I wasn't sure I'd be interested in him. He'd need more than a bunch of flowers to sort out this mess.

I tilted my head and breathed in deeply. The stench of overripe fruit, gone off meat, and stale beer filled my nose. My gaze shifted to the alleyway opposite us, and I caught a flash of scales and teeth.

"I've got something much more interesting than my old boyfriend to deal with," I said. "Do you smell that?"

Zandra lifted her nose and took a deep breath. "The overripe banana and gross meat smell?"

"That's our demon. Let's go have a good old-fashioned brawl with a bad guy."

"That might make you feel better after seeing Rhett ride off without even noticing you."

I almost growled at her. Instead, I channeled my anger into my magic. This poor sap of a demon wouldn't know what had hit him.

Chapter 2

"And the way you slammed your hand into Paxos' chest and ripped out his insides, that was epic." Zandra strode along beside me, shaking her head. "I take back everything I said about demon hunting. Although the hunting is boring, the slaying is awesome."

"It wasn't supposed to go down like that," I grumbled, although I was pleased Zandra was taking an interest in the demon hunting business. "He was supposed to come quietly. The job was to bag and tag the demon then hand him to Angel Force to process and charge."

"That's boring. And you don't want to be the angels' obedient little yes witch. You're an attack hound, like Wiggles, although much bigger and scarier."

"Wiggles can be scary, especially if you make a move on the last donut in the box when he's got his eye on it."

"Yeah, but you want demons quivering every time they hear the name Tempest Crypt. You want them running in the opposite direction and promising to behave so they never have to see you again. And what you just did to Paxos will get them talking. That's what will make you a legend."

"Who said anything about wanting to be a legend? I like a quiet life. I enjoy running my bar, keeping my head down, and not drawing attention."

"Does that include Rhett's attention?"

"Let's not mention we saw him," I said. "It'll only get the family talking, and I've got nothing to say about the situation. I don't know why he was in Mudacre. I don't know where he was headed, and I've no clue if he'll ever come back to Willow Tree Falls."

"He's an idiot for ditching you," Zandra said.

"He didn't ditch me," I muttered.

"Every guy must want a girlfriend who can smash through a demon with her bare hands."

I gave her a half-smile. My super-strength had been partially because of letting Frank's energy out. Plus, I'd been angry at Rhett, so I needed to let off steam. And once I'd cornered Paxos in the alleyway, he hadn't wanted to come quietly. Then he'd almost knocked Zandra's head off her shoulders with a bolt of magic, and I'd seen red.

But Zandra didn't need to know about Frank lending a hand in the demon pounding. He'd been stirring for months, slipping out of my control when I least expected it. And it was only a matter of time before he came to the boil and everything bubbled over into a huge sticky mess of chaos.

I was still working on a plan for what to do when that happened. So far, keeping quiet was the best I'd come up with.

"Will we still get paid, even though the demon's dead?" Zandra said. "We're splitting the money down the middle, right?"

"The evidence Paxos is no longer a problem is in this bag." I tapped the demon catching bag containing Paxos' heart. "We'll get two thirds of the pay because we didn't bring him back alive. I'll split it with you. You get one third."

"What? I did most of the work."

"You were busy looking at Rhett, rather than learning how to track a demon."

"Only because you were pretending you didn't care about seeing him. Admit it, you still like him."

"Here we are," I said as we passed through the magic barrier that surrounded Willow Tree Falls.

"You can't avoid the Rhett situation forever," Zandra said.

"I can try."

Wiggles bounded over. He blinked up at me and yawned. "What took you so long?"

"What do you mean? I said I'd be gone a few days." I bent and petted his head, always happy to see my furry little red-eyed buddy waiting for me.

He backed away. "Gross! You stink of demon."

"That's because Tempest shoved her hand inside Paxos' chest." Zandra thrust her hand out and twisted it at the wrist. "She ripped him apart because he wouldn't give himself up. It was great."

Wiggles' ears pricked. "What's got you in such a bad mood? You only go into destroy mode when you're tired, grumpy, or I've done something bad to the bed pillows. Which I absolutely haven't. I've barely sniffed them while you've been away.

Although I may have licked one. But only one. You'll barely notice when you get home."

"Leave my pillows unmolested," I said. "Zandra, why don't you drop off the demon remains at Angel Force?"

She backed away and wrinkled her nose. "No way. I need a shower, food, and some sleep."

"You're my assistant! Assistants do the boring jobs."

"You don't need to worry about going to see the angels. The scariest of the bunch is looking for you," Wiggles said. "Dazielle's been chasing me around and keeps asking where you are. And there's something weird about her."

"Weirder than usual?"

He nodded. "She's making me nervous. And even though I can take down an angel while eating a bear claw and sniffing an interesting dirt patch, I wouldn't like to tangle with Dazielle, given her weird mood."

"She knew I was hunting Paxos. She sent me on this job. She can't have forgotten about that."

"That's what I told her, but she wouldn't give up. I got so stressed about being hassled that I ate the whole carton of oatmeal cookies you left in the top cupboard, right at the back, behind the out-of-date jar of pickled onions and the ancient shaker of turmeric. And I don't even like oatmeal cookies."

"How did you... never mind." I shook my head. Wherever I hid the treats, Wiggles would find them. Even the ones he didn't like.

"I was comfort eating. Having a huge, angry angel chasing after you does nothing for my calm vibes.

Eek! Here she comes. Hide me." Wiggles jumped into my arms.

"What's wrong with you? You know Dazielle. Her bark is a lot worse than her bite." I sat him back on the ground.

"I'm getting out of here." Zandra's expression darkened as she stared at Dazielle, who was approaching us at speed.

"I'll catch up with you later," I said.

"You'd better. I want my cut of the money. You said fifty-fifty, right?"

I shook my head. "Go. Get some rest."

Zandra glanced at Dazielle one more time before scurrying away.

"Where have you been?" Dazielle jammed her hands on her hips and stared down at me from her impressive angel height, her wings beating behind her, stirring my hair around my face.

"Doing the job you told me to do. I didn't bring Paxos back alive, but I got you a nice souvenir. It used to beat. It's very sticky."

"I don't care about the demon. I have a much bigger problem on my hands."

"I told you she was acting weird." Wiggles peeked out from behind my legs.

I pursed my lips and tilted my head, giving Dazielle a good long look over. She did seem more stressed than normal. Her usually pristine blonde hair looked un-brushed, and her white blouse was misbuttoned.

"What's going on? What's more important than me catching Paxos?"

"You'll soon find out. Follow me." She turned and marched away.

"What do you think she'd do if I ignored her order?" I said to Wiggles. I was tired, stank of dead demon, and really needed some sleep.

"I heard that," Dazielle shot over her shoulder. "And you really don't want to push me, not today."

"You'd better follow the angel," Wiggles whispered. "I think she's lost her mind. Ever since all the other angels appeared, Dazielle's been walking around looking like the world is about to end."

"Other angels?" I hurried along with Wiggles.

"There are so many of them. They started appearing from the sky two days ago, not long after you left."

"Hey, Dazielle! Wait up." I broke into a jog to keep up with her large strides.

"I don't have time to wait. You have to help me fix this problem."

"What's the problem? Is there a demon loose in the village?"

"This has nothing to do with demons, but I am being plagued by a terrifying problem."

"A plague?" Wiggles bared his teeth. "Will it infect me? Does it come from fleas? I've heard bad things about fleas and plagues. Tempest, I don't usually ask for a bath, but in this case—"

"Not an actual plague." Dazielle fluffed out her wings.

"Does this problem have anything to do with the extra angels in the village?" I said.

"Yes! I didn't expect them all to turn up early, but they wanted to enjoy our spas and the stone circle. And they keep showing up at the office and at my apartment and congratulating me. It's awful."

"It sounds like torture. Why don't you want them congratulating you?"

She swiped her wings through the air. "They expect me to be happy about what's about to happen. How can I be happy?"

"I'm lost. Maybe buy me a coffee and explain this in simple language."

"There's no time for coffee."

I looked down at Wiggles and shrugged. "Has an angel convention showed up you weren't expecting? Or is it an inspection?"

Dazielle groaned. "It's my mom. She's brought forward my marriage."

"Oh! That's not good. When's it happening?"

"In two days."

I stopped walking, and my mouth fell open. "You can't plan a wedding in such a short amount of time."

"No, of course you can't." Dazielle gestured at me to keep walking. "Especially not an angel wedding. But Mom's been planning this day for most of my life. And it's been arranged since I was a child. She's worked on the finishing touches for the last two years."

"The last two years! This sounds like it'll be a posh, expensive affair."

Dazielle's shoulders slumped. "It has to be. It's what's expected of my family. Mom's done with me making excuses, so she arranged everything. She sent out the invitations, picked the venue, ordered the food. It's all organized."

"Your mom did all of that without telling you?"

"She told me plenty of times this was what she'd do if I didn't get a date in the diary to marry Gadreel, but I didn't think she'd go through with it."

"And you can't stand Gadreel, right?"

Dazielle nodded. "Our joining was determined when we were infants. It's been the way our families have done things for thousands of years. My line is a noble line of angels, and we marry to secure alliances."

"You don't love the person you marry?"

"It's rarely about love. It's about duty and honor."

I widened my eyes at Wiggles, and he snorted out smoke. What was I supposed to do about Dazielle's mess? "I mean, that's not much fun, but if that's the way you've always done things and you agreed to it, what's with the big freak out?"

Dazielle turned, grabbed my shoulders, and shook me so hard my teeth rattled. "I can't marry smug Gadreel in two days' time. I always figured I'd find a workaround, a way to convince my mom I shouldn't marry him. He's such a... such a..."

"Giant douche bag?"

She nodded. "The biggest. I mean, he's handsome enough. He's an angel and comes from a fine breeding stock."

"You make him sound like a horse," I said.

Wiggles made a braying sound and tossed his fake mane as he cantered around us.

"You know what I mean." Dazielle glared at Wiggles until he stopped cantering and slunk away.

"It's not about his looks. His personality is awful. He's so self-satisfied and struts around like he owns the place."

I grinned up at her. "It sounds like you're describing yourself. You should get along well. Maybe this wedding isn't a mistake."

She shoved me away and kept walking. "I'm nothing like Gadreel. I care about other people. I care about Willow Tree Falls. And I don't want this marriage to change things."

"What'll change just because you change your name to Mrs. Gadreel McSmug and have a huge rock on your finger? It will be a big gemstone in your wedding ring, won't it? I imagine you're a diamond kind of angel. You love anything that sparkles."

"It can be a lump of fossilized dinosaur poop for all I care. Once I marry, my role will have to change. What if I have to leave Angel Force?"

"Your husband can't make you do that. This is the modern age. Once you're married, you don't give up everything and tie yourself to the kitchen sink."

"Gadreel is... difficult. And his family is traditional. They'll expect things from me. I'll have to attend high-profile events, travel more, and have lots of children." She made a gagging sound in the back of her throat. "Just the thought of Gadreel touching me makes me want to vomit."

"I, um, well, like I said, it sucks to be you, but why are you telling me this?" I looked around and leaned closer. "Do you want me to hunt Gadreel down and chase him out of the village? I've never killed an angel, but for the right price—"

She whirled around and grabbed me again so tightly I yelped. "You'd do that for me? You'd assassinate a high profile angel to give me back my freedom?"

"No! Dazielle, I was joking." I wriggled in her grip. She'd lifted me off the ground, and my feet dangled in the air. "Quit with the grabbing, or Frank will get interested in you. You know how much he loves fighting with angels."

She lowered me to the ground. "Frank! He could help. We could say you lost control of him and lopped off Gadreel's head. Yes! That would work. You'd only get ten to fifteen years in prison if I supported your claim for diminished responsibility."

"Dazielle, we might be sort of buddies, but I'm not killing your fiancé. If you want him dead, you kill him."

She spat out an exasperated sigh. "Then we stick to my original plan. You have to help me make preparations."

I held up my hands. "You're talking to the wrong Crypt witch. There's no way I can help you prepare for a big wedding in two days. I know nothing about getting married. Speak to Aurora. She's the queen of weddings. She had an amazing ceremony with Lex. He might even let you have rooms in the castle for your guests."

"No! I don't need your help in picking out my dress or dealing with venues. All that's sorted."

"And once again, I'm completely lost. You need to let me inside your head. How am I supposed to help you get married?"

"That's exactly it. You're not. I've figured out a way to stop the wedding from happening, but I need you to convince the other party to be involved."

"The other party? Who are we talking about?"

Dazielle caught hold of my arm and hauled me to the Angel Force building. She marched through the doors, ignored the angel on the reception desk, and headed straight into the offices.

Several angels tried to stop her, holding up files for her attention. She waved them all away. "Not now. I'm dealing with a crisis." She marched past them all and stopped outside a closed interview room.

Wiggles caught up with us, his tongue hanging out. "Dazielle's been charging around like this ever since you left."

"There's a good reason I've been charging around," Dazielle said. "In here." She opened the door just wide enough so I could get in with Wiggles.

I shuffled in and looked around. The only odd thing in the room was that Dominic occupied one of the chairs. And he looked miserable. Dominic was the most cheerful angel I knew.

"Hey! How's it going? Have you got a new job yet?"

He shook his head and pointed at his mouth.

Dazielle came in behind me and shut the door with a bang.

"Are you involved in this wedding plan?" I asked Dominic.

His eyes widened, and he opened his mouth, but no sound came out.

"Have you lost your voice?"

He shook his head and tilted it at Dazielle.

I crossed my arms over my chest and turned to her. "What have you done? Why can't Dominic speak?"

"I had to keep him quiet. I didn't want him telling anyone what I have planned. You know how terrible he is at keeping secrets."

I looked back at Dominic. He was gripping the arms of the chair, his whole body shaking. There were pizza stains down the front of his white shirt. "Have you kidnapped him?"

Dazielle tutted. "It's not kidnapping. He's a full grown angel. And he came willingly. Well, he did to begin with. It was only when I explained my plan that he grew anxious. I had to make sure he understood everything. And I couldn't risk him getting away now he knows the truth."

"So you trapped him in this chair and took away his voice?" I said.

Dazielle swooped her wings behind her. "It's a temporary thing."

I stood in front of Dominic, feeling the need to protect him from Dazielle, given how manic she was being. "Release him from whatever magic is holding him. I need to hear his side of the story."

Dazielle narrowed her eyes then leaned around me. She jabbed a finger at Dominic. "If you make a run for it, I'll hunt you down and pluck every feather from your wings. Do you understand me?"

Dominic shook in his seat before nodding.

Dazielle moved to the back of the chair. She placed her hands on either side of Dominic's head, and a silver aura pulsed over him. "You're released from my binding."

Dominic let out a gasp and jumped from the chair. He backed away from Dazielle. "Tempest, you must help me. She's lost her mind."

"I don't disagree with you," I said. "But why are you involved?"

He fell to his knees and clutched my hands. "Because she wants to marry me."

Chapter 3

My gaze cut from Dominic, who was shaking so much he could barely draw breath, back to Dazielle, who stood with her wings extended and her hands clasped in front of her.

"Let's go back about a thousand steps. Dazielle, why does Dominic think you're going to get married?" I said.

"Because we are. At least that's what I'm going to tell my mom," Dazielle said.

"You don't even like Dominic. You can't get married."

He nodded vigorously. "It's true. Dazielle fired me because I couldn't keep a secret, and she was always telling me I was incompetent. Do you remember how much she hated it when I color-coded things in the office?" He glanced at Dazielle then ducked his head. "You don't like a single thing about me."

"You also annoy the heck out of me because you don't have a brain inside that head of yours," Dazielle said. "But if you'd listened to a word I'd said to you, you'd know what I actually had planned."

I helped Dominic to his feet, and he stood behind me, his hands on my shoulders like I was his shield, protecting him from Dazielle.

"Did you trap Dominic in this room because you want to force him into a marriage?"

Dazielle hesitated. "Yes and no. There'll be no forcing of any marriages. I'm not marrying Dominic, and I'm certainly not marrying Gadreel."

"So what's the plan?"

"I'm going to convince my mom that Dominic and I are in love."

"I don't love you!" he whispered, his tone filled with horror.

"And I don't love you," Dazielle said. "But it's the only way I can get the real wedding stopped. I need to make Mom see sense and support my plan to marry for love and not because it creates an alliance between two angel factions."

"But you told me love isn't a factor when you get married," I said.

"And how awful does that sound?" Dazielle's wings drooped. "I always thought I wouldn't mind when it came to it. My parents joined because their alliance worked for both families. My sisters have done the same. But..."

"Their marriages aren't happy?"

"One of my sisters spends a lot of time away from her husband. And they have no children. She once confessed to me they sleep in separate rooms. It sounded awful."

"Yeah, but it's a marriage of convenience, not a marriage of lust and romance."

"Don't I deserve a marriage of lust and romance? I'm an attractive angel, I have prospects, and I'm an excellent cook." Dazielle smoothed a hand over her hair.

"I'm not saying any of that's not true, but why do you think telling your mom you've fallen for Dominic will change her mind about your marriage to Gadreel?"

"Because she sees how miserable my sisters are. She must have a heart. And I know my father isn't the kindest of angels. He's not around often. Mom prefers it that way."

"What's Gadreel got to make him such a catch, alliance wise? Isn't there someone else you could marry and form a useful alliance with? Someone you don't hate? Maybe even someone you think is cute."

"No one is as well-connected as Gadreel." Dazielle rubbed her forehead. "And there have been a few... skirmishes. They must be squashed."

"The angels are fighting? What about?"

Dazielle stiffened, and her eyes flickered with irritation. "It's not witch business."

I shrugged and turned to the door. "I thought you wanted my help."

"No! Stay!" Dominic wrapped his arms around me, wrapping me in a tight bear hug from behind. "Don't leave me with Dazielle."

I patted his arm. "Relax. I don't want my ribs getting snapped."

He let go but clung to my shoulders again and leaned in close. "There's a power struggle at the top."

"Dominic! Angel business shouldn't be gossiped about."

"That's no way to speak to your new husband-to-be. You must respect each other if you're going to make this relationship last."

Dazielle scowled at me. "Are you going to joke about this, or will you help us?"

"I'm considering my options. You've got to admit it's kind of ridiculous."

"My life isn't ridiculous. It's complicated." Dazielle stared at the floor.

I huffed out a breath, feeling a little bad for finding her situation funny. I also got the complicated issue, so I wasn't about to abandon them just yet. "Tell me more about your mom. She sounds like she's using her daughters to gain power. Does that sound about right?"

"Mom can be.... power hungry."

"She's the biggest social climber I've ever met," Dominic whispered.

Dazielle flared out her wings, and he cringed away. She lowered them and sighed. "Hester, my mom, mainly cares about how people see her."

I tilted my head. "Like mother, like daughter?"

"I'm not like that!"

"Please, help me," Dominic said. "I can't be married to an angel with a temper."

"How did you persuade Dominic to come here?" I asked. "You kicked him out of Angel Force, so he owes you nothing."

"That's not important." Dazielle shuffled her wings back into place. "All that matters is he's here, and he'll go along with my plan."

I turned and faced Dominic. "What did Dazielle do to get you here?"

"Um... she promised she'd reinstate me if I lied about being in love with her."

"I didn't use the word *promise*, and I never told you to lie about anything," Dazielle said. "Angels rarely lie."

"You making up a whole relationship with Dominic is telling the truth?" Dazielle could be one sneaky angel when she needed to be.

"I... I... we had an agreement. Dominic said he would help me."

He ducked his head. "I'm not sure I can go through with it. It's too scary."

"You must!"

"And if he doesn't? Dazielle, you can't keep Dominic trapped in this room and pretend there's a relationship going on. Your mom won't believe that. She'll know something is wrong." I stood between them, not liking the angry expression on Dazielle's face. "I tell you what, let's get out of here and find neutral ground so we can talk this out. And I'm starving. Demon hunting takes it out of you. How about we grab breakfast?"

"I'm too stressed to eat," Dazielle said.

"I could eat." Dominic brushed a hand down his stained shirt. "Although I've been overindulging since I lost my job, so I'm not in the best of shape." He flexed a toned bicep.

"You look in great shape to me," I said.

"Angels have high metabolisms, but I won't have a fat groom," Dazielle said. "No donuts for breakfast, only fruit."

"You'll have no groom if you keep being rude. Let's go give those high metabolisms a workout. We'll go to Sprinkles. Patti has set up some new seating inside, so we can find somewhere quiet." I headed to the door and looked over my shoulder. "Or if you two lovers want to stay here and work out your differences with a little rough and tumble, that's fine by me."

Dominic's cheeks flushed a deep red, and he shook his head.

"Let's go," Dazielle said. "But no funny business, Dominic. If you run, I'll catch you and make you pay."

I grinned. "You really do like to play rough, Dazielle."

"I just want to go home," Dominic muttered. "I don't feel good."

"You stick with me." I eased my arm through his elbow and tugged him close to my side. "I won't let mean old Dazielle do anything to you. Although it sounds like she's in the mood for kiss and chase."

He shuddered. "No more teasing, please."

We dashed to Sprinkles, placed our order, and settled at a table out of the way of anyone else.

Dazielle groaned and hid her face in her hands. "There's Gadreel swaggering past like a prize peacock on steroids."

"Which one is he?" I peered at a group of perfect looking angels strolling past the bakery.

"Gadreel's the tall one with the shoulder-length blond hair and the dazzling teeth," Dominic said.

I wasn't into the clean-cut look, but the angel he pointed out had it going on. Gadreel had broad shoulders, full lips, and bright blue eyes. "Are you sure you don't want to marry him, Dazielle? He's a ten on the drool factor."

She wrinkled her nose as she peered through her fingers. "If you want him, you're welcome to him. And looks aren't everything."

I studied Gadreel as he strutted along the street, acknowledging people with a nod of his head and a toss of his thick wavy hair. "No, he's not for me. He seems too full of himself."

"And that's Dazielle's mom, Hester." Dominic pointed to a stunning mature angel with silvery blonde hair that fell to her waist. Her wings had stripes of gold and silver running through them.

"Whoa! That's your mom? I can feel her power from here."

"Don't stare, or she'll notice you," Dazielle said. "Mom has an... instinct for spotting trouble."

"And she's terrifying," Dominic said. "I heard she strode straight into the Angel Force office and took over when she arrived. All the angels were running around helping her."

Dazielle sighed. "Mom has that effect on people. She's been around a long time and has gathered power and influence. And she continues to gather it. That's why she wants me to marry Gadreel. His parents are almost as powerful as her. Although they're new power. They've only been around a thousand years."

Our food arrived, and we all took a moment to enjoy the chocolate chip muffins and warm almond croissants.

"Dazielle! Shouldn't you be making preparations?" An angel with an adorable blonde pixie cut and a wide smile on her pretty face rushed over. She was with a slightly shorter, curvier female angel.

Dazielle tensed in her seat. "Irin! I don't need to worry about a thing. Mom's got it all in hand."

"Of course she has. She never changes." Irin looked around the table. "Who are your friends?"

Dazielle narrowed her eyes at me, as if warning me to watch myself. "This is Tempest Crypt. Her family looks after the demon prison in the village. And this is Dominic. He... he works for me. This is Irin and Lailah. Lailah will officiate my wedding to Gadreel." She almost choked on his name.

"It's good to meet you both," I said. "Dazielle's been filling me in on the news. I've been away for a couple of days, so I've missed the wedding excitement."

"Yes! Isn't it exciting?" Irin said. "I must admit I was beginning to think I'd never see the day when my old friend walked along the aisle."

"You two have known each other a long time?"

"We were in school together. I know all of Dazielle's secrets." Irin grinned. "Although she also knows all of mine, so I'll never tell." Her gaze drifted to Dominic, and her eyes sparked with interest.

"We don't have any secrets," Dazielle muttered.

"Are you looking forward to the ceremony?" I asked.

Lailah nodded. "Oh, yes. I enjoy a wedding. It'll be my six hundred and twelfth ceremony."

"That's a ton of weddings to take care of. You never get bored?"

She shook her head. "I enjoyed each one."

"Angel weddings are such fun," Irin said. "And this will be a huge social event. I've heard there could even be representation from a higher angel." She glanced at my forehead then looked away.

"Mom's been trying to convince a higher angel to come," Dazielle said. "She shouldn't waste her time. They have more important things to do than see me get married to Gadreel."

"No! This is serious business. Once your families are joined, you'll be unstoppable. And I heard Gadreel was talking about buying a property in some far-off magical place. He mentioned a beach resort with mountains. Imagine that. You can rule your own fairy castle. He'd better make sure you have one with turrets."

I grinned and nudged Dominic as Irin continued to twitter on. Dazielle sort of smiled, but it looked strained. Maybe they weren't such good friends, after all.

"I don't like to break up the fun, but we should go," Lailah said. "I'd like another look around the venue, and Hester has asked to see me again."

"Sorry! I hope she's not causing you too much trouble," Dazielle said. "Don't let her be too demanding. It's just a wedding."

"Your mother is fine. She's an angel who knows her mind, and that's appreciated. I have so many couples who change things at the last second, but your mother knows exactly what she wants. I'm happy to assist her in any way I can."

"She does know her own mind." Dazielle glanced at me and frowned.

Irin looked at Dominic again, her eyes full of appreciation, despite the croissant crumbs on his shirt. "I hope you're not tempted by this handsome angel. You'd better not be having second thoughts about getting married to Gadreel."

Dazielle sat bolt upright and dropped her fork. "Of course not. I mean..."

Irin laughed. "I'm teasing. You're so stressed. Although you will be the center of attention in front of hundreds of influential angels in two days' time. I'd probably be sweating a little, too. Although we prefer to call it glowing."

"Dazielle has been glowing loads," I said.

She stood on my foot under the table and pressed down.

"It's lovely to meet you all. We must have a dance when we're at the ceremony." Irin glanced at Dominic again and winked.

"I look forward to it," I said.

Irin and Lailah walked over to the counter and placed their order.

I continued to eat my muffin as I mulled over the upcoming wedding. I felt sorry for Dominic and Dazielle, but this was her mess. And I had my own family issues and a tricky relationship to sort out. This angel love triangle had nothing to do with me.

"Do you see my problem?" Dazielle said. "Everyone thinks this marriage to Gadreel is the right thing to do."

"Maybe this is a case of cold feet. Don't force Dominic to do something you'll both regret. Let him go and get on with the wedding," I said.

Dazielle's lips thinned. "I can't."

"You can. And Gadreel might be decent when you get to know him and you get used to living a life of luxury in your castle."

"You will help me, Tempest. Gadreel is the wrong angel for me. I'll be miserable, and I could lose everything. I refuse to take that risk."

"So don't take the risk but leave innocent parties out of this mess. Set Dominic free and figure out another way to break off your engagement."

She thumped a hand on the table. "You're going to help me."

I lowered my mug, not liking the evil look in her eyes. "Or what?"

Dazielle raised her chin, her pale blue eyes glinting. "Or I'll bring Zandra in for questioning."

"Questioning about what, exactly?"

"I'm aware she's been misusing magic. I've spoken to you about this, and you assured me you had everything in hand. That's not the case. Zandra continues to bend the rules. She's using spells way beyond her control, and it concerns me that she could be a danger to others."

"Zandra is none of your concern. Leave her out of this."

Dazielle shook her head. "I can't do that. In fact, I'll send an angel out today to bring Zandra in. I can speak to her about the problem she has with magic. Although..."

"Go on, say it. Show me just how deceitful angels can really be." I leaned toward her, anger sparking through me.

"I might forget all about Zandra's indiscretions if you help me."

Dominic shook his head. "Dazielle, that's not fair."

"Who cares about fair? I'm desperate."

I jabbed a finger at her. "You sneaky angel. Why are we even friends? You're always blackmailing me or threatening to arrest a member of my family. I should tell Granny Dottie about this. Maybe she'll let a few of the demons out of the prison. Then we can sit back and see how the angels handle that problem without our help."

Dazielle grasped my hand, a strangled sob coming out of her mouth. "I can't marry Gadreel."

I stuffed my last bite of muffin into my mouth and chewed, glaring at Dazielle as I did so. "I'll help you, but don't you dare go anywhere near Zandra. I'm looking out for her. That's all you need to know."

"And so long as you help me stay unmarried, the Zandra matter goes no further."

I scowled at her, not liking how easily she'd played me. "Then you'd better sign me up as your un-wedding planner."

Chapter 4

"I don't believe we've been introduced."

The silky smooth feminine voice behind me had the hairs standing up on the back of my neck.

Dazielle jumped out of her seat, knocking it over in her haste. "Mother! What are you doing here?"

"I suspect the same thing as you." The stunning, silvery blonde-haired angel Dominic had pointed out to me appeared in my view. She pressed a brief kiss on Dazielle's cheek. Her ice-blue gaze settled on Dominic and then me. Her gaze drifted up to my forehead. "We've not met. I'm Hester."

I wiped my fingers on a napkin and then shook her outstretched hand. "Tempest Crypt. I've been hearing about the wedding plans."

Hester grasped my hand. She yanked me to my feet and ran her fingers across my forehead. "You're the witch marked by the higher angels. I've heard about you."

There was no point trying to struggle out of her grip. Hester could easily snap my wrist without breaking a sweat. "I've had dealings with them a time or two."

"So I've heard." Her gaze intensified. "A witch with influence among the angels is rare. You must be important."

"Mom! Tempest is a friend. And you know about the Crypt family. They keep the demons in check."

Hester dismissed her daughter's comment with a wave of her hand. "An angel mark is valuable and important. I trust you're using it well. The higher angels don't give these marks out lightly. They expect the guardian of such a mark to respect the power they've been bestowed."

I stepped back so Hester could no longer stroke my forehead. This up close and personal with her was weird. "I barely remember it's there if I'm being honest."

Hester dropped her hold on my hand. "I'm glad you're not abusing your gift."

"Nope. I have zero plans to do any gift abusing."

Hester's top lip curled a fraction, then a calm smile crossed her face. "Of course. And as a friend of my daughter, I'm assured you have an esteemed reputation. Dazielle is always careful when picking her friends."

"I'm as esteemed as they come." I glanced at Dazielle, who was visibly shaking.

Hester looked at Dominic again but didn't introduce herself to him. "This is not what I expected to see just before your wedding, Dazielle. You should be in quiet contemplation, preparing yourself for a future with your new husband."

"I... um, Mom, about that."

"I have yet to convince a higher angel to come to the ceremony." Hester glanced at me. "Perhaps you could pull a few strings and get in touch with your connections, convince them to attend the ceremony. This joining will be important for many angels."

I shook my head. "I'm not sure that's a good idea. You know how busy these higher angels get. Doing important... err... higher angel business things."

She pursed her lips. "This alliance is of interest to them. The higher angels must see we're working for the greater good by creating this coupling. And Gadreel is in negotiations to acquire another enchanted cottage complex. If the deal goes through, his wealth will vastly increase."

"Mom, I don't care how wealthy Gadreel is," Dazielle stammered.

"Of course you do, darling. We don't marry poor. Now, I have the Clover Hill angels attending and the Silver Star angels. Every single member. They must be in the first five rows of the ceremony so they can see how much money has been spent. Sophia snubbed one of my suggestions at a committee meeting and said I didn't have the talent to fulfill my duty. This will show her exactly what I can achieve."

"Can't the guests sit where they like?" Dazielle's pleading gaze turned my way.

"Don't be ridiculous. This is a day everyone must remember for a long time."

Dazielle looked like she was about to burst into tears. I should leave her hanging after the stunt she'd pulled, but I had agreed to help her.

"Gadreel's wrong for Dazielle," I said.

Hester blinked once and pulled herself up to her full height. She was even taller than Dazielle. "What do you mean? Gadreel is perfection. He's wealthy, his family has all the right connections, and he's handsome. And two powerful families uniting will solve any... problems that might arise."

"You mean the angel skirmishes?" I said.

Hester glanced at Dazielle, her features sharpening.

"I haven't said a word, Mom."

I tapped my forehead. "I'm in with the right angels. I hear things."

"Of course." Hester's tinkling laugh made my spine stiffen. "You do know the higher angels well if they're discussing our in-fighting with you. It's not something we're proud of, but this alliance could help."

Dazielle lowered into her seat and clasped her mug of coffee.

"Don't you feel weird about sending your daughter off to marry some guy she doesn't want to be with?"

Hester jerked back as if I'd struck her. "Gadreel's very nice. Of course, she wants to be with him."

"I'm sure he's someone's ideal angel, but have you asked Dazielle if she's into him? Does she find him attractive? Maybe she doesn't like him."

"Like him! That's irrelevant."

"Does your other daughter say that when she's alone in her bed at night and her husband is off doing who knows what with who knows whom?"

"He... he doesn't do that!" Hester glanced down at Dazielle. "What has Simitri been saying? I know there have been a few squabbles, but it's nothing serious."

Dazielle bit her lip. "It's more than a squabble. Simitri is miserable."

"She's never mentioned her marriage is making her unhappy." Hester's wings fluttered. "I must deal with that matter but after your wedding."

"The wedding that could make another of your daughters distraught?" I said.

"Tempest, now's not the right time," Dazielle whispered. "Sorry, Mom. Of course, I'll marry Gadreel if it'll make you happy. And I understand it needs to happen. I just thought... it doesn't matter what I thought."

Hester looked from me to Dazielle. Her gaze ran over her daughter several times. "Wait, just wait a moment. I'm interested in what this witch is saying. But you must understand, we marry for—"

"Alliances and connections. I know that. But doesn't it feel emotionally hollow? Why not let one of your daughters marry for love? You've got the others married off in positions of power. How much power do you need?"

"What kind of question is that? We need to stay relevant. The social status is always changing as new alliances are formed. If you don't have a clear, powerful family in charge, problems arise."

"Maybe some of these problems arise because the alliances make angels cold and unfeeling. They're fighting with other groups of angels because their personal lives are devoid of joy and affection. How's your marriage doing, Hester?"

"Tempest! That's enough," Dazielle hissed.

"No! I want to know what's going on," Hester said stiffly. "And my marriage is fine. Thank you for asking."

"What if Dazielle married for love?" I said. "That would be a demonstration of your strength. You're showing others that you don't need to join forces with anyone else because you're already so powerful. That would be novel. It would get other angels talking, so you'd get plenty of attention. And I'm sure the higher angels would be interested in such an unusual approach to diplomacy."

Hester leaned down and peered intently into my eyes. Tiny silver sparkles drifted out of her mouth every time she exhaled. "Do you really think they would?"

I nodded, although I had no idea if they'd give a flying fig about who Dazielle married. "They're bored with seeing the same old alliances. Angels need love, too. Isn't that what you're all about, making wishes come true?"

"You're mistaking us for genies." Hester glanced at Dazielle again. "It would be unusual, and it would draw attention to us."

"Mom, I really would like to marry for love," Dazielle said. "And I promise, I'll do all the interviews and attend all the events you want me to, so I can show off my new husband. Whatever it takes. Please, don't make me marry Gadreel."

"This could just work in our favor." Hester tapped a finger against her chin.

"And where there's true love, there are often babies. Wouldn't you like a crib full of adorable angel babies to play with?" I ignored the kick Dazielle gave me.

Hester's eyes sparkled. "Yes, I'd like that very much. My other children have been slow to provide grandbabies."

"Then we have a solution. Call off the wedding to Gadreel, and Dazielle can marry for love when the time is right."

"Not so fast. You talk about a love match, but you've made no mention of who you actually want to marry." Hester's gaze was lasered to Dazielle. "You must have someone in mind."

I looked at Dominic. He shook in his seat, his gaze pinned to his plate. It was time for him to play his part. "He's right here. Dominic, meet Hester, your future mother-in-law."

Dominic stood, pushed out his chest, and gave Hester his most dazzling smile. "It's a pleasure to meet you."

Hester took his hand and held it between both of hers, her sharp gaze sparking. "You wish to marry my daughter?"

Dominic swallowed but nodded. I couldn't have been more proud of him. He must be terrified from being confronted by so much power, but he was holding his own.

"I do. I've known Dazielle for a long time. She's a... a decent angel. And she's pretty when she smiles."

"And this match, Tempest," Hester said, her gaze going to the mark on my forehead again. "Do you believe the higher angels will bless this? They will see a love match as an asset?"

"Sure. I approve of it, so I'm certain the higher angels will. Plus, it will make Dazielle happy."

"Yes, of course. Well, this is most unconventional." Hester studied Dominic. "You're a handsome enough angel, and you'd look perfect standing beside Dazielle. But it's so sudden. Are you both ready for this commitment?"

"Yes!" Dazielle hopped from her seat and stood beside her mom. "I'm so ready. When you brought forward my wedding to Gadreel, I had to act. I need to be with someone I love. And... I love Dominic."

"I'm still not sure. There's so much to think about," Hester said.

"You don't have to think about anything," I said. "I'm sure this match will work out great."

Hester took hold of Dazielle's hand and then Dominic's and placed them together. She rested her hand on top of theirs. "You have my blessing. You may be together. I'll allow this change."

Dominic and Dazielle heaved out huge sighs.

"Thanks, Mom. You don't know how much this means to me," Dazielle said.

"I think I do. I'm not the tyrant everyone makes me out to be, and I recognize there is more to a marriage than a simple alliance. And I have a good feeling about this one." Hester patted Dominic's cheek. "It's all agreed. You will marry Dominic instead. I'm about to speak with Lailah, so I'll make the changes to the vows and the licence while I'm with her. If I'm quick, I can get it pushed through this morning, so you'll have nothing to worry about. Leave everything to me. Oh, and Dominic, I hope you have a suitable tuxedo. You need to look your best if you're to join this family."

Dominic stammered out some unintelligible noises, his cheeks paler than his wing feathers.

"So charming." Hester patted his cheek again. "I must go. I have so many changes to make before the ceremony takes place." She flew out of Sprinkles.

I stared at the spot Hester had been standing. "Um... congratulations, you two."

Dazielle dropped into her seat with a groan.

Dominic stayed standing, swaying from side to side. "Did... did that just happen? It was going so well. Your mom thinks we're getting married for real?"

I eased Dominic into a seat before he fainted. "It did. But at least Dazielle is off the hook for marrying Gadreel."

Dazielle groaned again. "That wasn't meant to happen. I don't want to marry Dominic. What are we supposed to do now? Mom will make all the changes and simply substitute Dominic for Gadreel. I'm back where I started."

I grinned as I settled in my seat and grabbed Dazielle's abandoned muffin off her plate. "Beats me. But it looks like you two are getting wed."

⁂

"Please don't mess this up," Dominic said. He stood under the porch of the wedding chapel, shaking from head to toe in an incredibly white tuxedo.

I dabbed sweat off his brow with a hankie. "Relax. Everything is sorted. I'll make sure the wedding stops before you say the vows and have to smooch Dazielle. We've gone over this loads of times. Nothing will go wrong."

"I should leave now. You could tell everyone I got cold feet and ran away." He turned toward the exit.

I caught hold of his arm and held him in place. "And then what would happen? You'd spend the rest of your life on the run while Hester hunted you down for abandoning Dazielle at the altar."

"Hester will hate you for messing with the wedding. What if she comes after you?" Dominic's bottom lip trembled. "Tempest, I've always liked you. I don't want anything bad to happen to you."

I patted his arm. "And I like you. That's why I'm doing this."

"No! I mean, I... I really like you. I know you don't see me that way, but I wouldn't mind getting married today if it was you waiting for me."

I shook my head and pointed to the chapel. He was such a sweet angel. Way too sweet for me. I'd eat him alive. "Focus on your bride-to-be. And I don't mind taking the heat for this. I can always say the higher angels changed their minds and don't approve of you or Gadreel being Dazielle's life partner. If Hester comes for me, I'll be ready for her."

"What if Hester finds out the truth?" Dominic said. "Do you really have regular chats with the higher angels about who's dating each other?"

"Of course not." I tapped my forehead. "But apparently, this mark means I could if I wanted to. And if things really go wrong, I will call on them for help. Maybe the higher angels want to see Dazielle in love and happy with someone, rather than shackled to the smug Gadreel."

He lifted one shoulder and licked his lips. "You could be right, and you know them better than me."

"Just go through the motions, say the words, and I'll interrupt at the right time."

Dominic gulped but nodded. "I'd better go in. Dazielle is waiting for me."

I straightened his bowtie. "By the end of the day, we'll be laughing about this over a large shot of lemon drop."

"I'll need several after this experience."

"And you'll get them. Off you go."

Angel weddings worked in reverse to most other weddings. The bride waited for the groom, so it was up to poor Dominic to hurry up the aisle on his own.

I watched him for a few seconds then eased the door almost closed so I could hear the vows.

"You think you're better than me."

I turned as I heard Zandra's raised voice outside the chapel.

"I don't! I'm just saying, you're spending a lot of time together." That was Aurora.

I looked down at Wiggles. "Don't take your eyes off the ceremony. Come get me the second they get to the important bit. I can't miss my cue."

He nodded. "I'm on it."

I walked away from the chapel door and headed outside. My sisters stood toe-to-toe, glaring at each other.

"Hey, what's going on?" I hurried over to them.

"Zandra's being a pig," Aurora said.

"Aurora! Calm down." I rarely heard her say anything mean about anyone. "What happened?"

Zandra jabbed a finger into Aurora's shoulder. "She told me I was lying when I said we'd been on a demon hunting mission."

"You are lying! Tempest wouldn't take you. You're untrained. You're dangerous."

I eased my arm between them and gently shoved them apart. "Take it down a notch. Aurora, I did take Zandra out with me. I'm teaching her how to hunt demons to see if it's a career she'd be interested in. What's the big deal?"

Aurora glared at me. "You never let me come out with you."

"Because you don't like demons, you have a store to run. And also, Frank."

"But... but..." She gestured at Zandra.

"But I'm better at hunting demons than you." Zandra's tone was smug.

"Quit being bratty. No one is better than anyone else. What's gotten in to you two?"

"I was fine until Zandra started muscling in," Aurora said.

"What's she muscling in on?" I said.

"Oh! You know!" Aurora wriggled her fingers at me.

"I really don't."

"I'm done with this. Family is more trouble than it's worth." Zandra turned and stomped away.

"We're only half-family," Aurora yelled.

"That was mean, Aurora." I shook my head at her. "I still don't understand what happened. Why were you fighting? I thought you liked Zandra."

"I don't. And you're the worst big sister in the world. You're useless." Tears sprung into Aurora's eyes before she marched away, too.

What just made my sisters act like children?

I turned and dashed back to the chapel. Just as I reached the door, my stomach dropped as I heard the ominous words, "You may now kiss the bride."

I gulped in a breath. "Wiggles! You were supposed to tell me when they asked if anyone objected. That was my cue to stop this." I peered through the door, just as Dominic pressed a quick kiss to Dazielle's lips, his wings hanging limp down his back.

"I got swept up in the moment and didn't want the ceremony to stop. Besides, Dazielle and Dominic look great together. I reckon it's true love. They just don't know it yet."

I stared with wide eyes through the crack in the door as the wedding march music began. This was terrible. I'd promised Dominic I wouldn't let him down. Now, he was married to his former boss, a boss who'd fired him for being a gossipy, incompetent airhead.

"Now the boring bit's over, let's get some angel food cake and party with the feathers," Wiggles said.

I had a feeling this would be anything but a fun party. If I didn't end up being pulled apart by the unhappy newlyweds, it would be a miracle.

Chapter 5

"This is great," Wiggles said from underneath the table. He'd wedged himself between my knees so he had easy access to the food I kept passing him.

I wasn't having such a good time and was too tense to eat. I kept shooting glances at the top table where Dazielle and Dominic sat, looking like uptight mannequins as they looked at everything but each other.

Dazielle caught my eye, and the glare she shot me was loaded with venom. I'd been getting death glares ever since she'd walked along the aisle with her new husband on her arm.

I wanted to tell her it wasn't my fault, and I'd had a family crisis to deal with, but it kind of was. I'd assured them I'd make sure they didn't get married, and now we were surrounded by hundreds of overexcited angels and friends of the bride and groom as they toasted their long-lasting love and happiness.

It was a disaster. Although I hoped Dazielle would eventually see the funny side, and maybe they could figure out a way to get along.

"Have you got any more of those lobster tails in butter?" Wiggles whispered. "They make me belch, but they're tasty."

"No belching anywhere near the wedding party." I passed him another lobster tail.

"When's the dancing starting?" Granny Dottie sat to my right. Auntie Queenie was to my left, along with my mom, my dad, and the rest of the family. Although Zandra and Aurora were absent.

"It should be any minute now," Grandpa Lucius said. "I'm looking forward to a boogie. I'll show these angels a thing or two."

"We can out dance those feathers," Granny Dottie said. "Pass me another glass of champagne, Tempest. I'm parched."

I grabbed a glass from a passing server.

"Are you sure that's such a good idea?" my mom said. "That's your sixth glass."

"Who's counting when it's a wedding?" Granny Dottie chuckled as she sipped on the bubbles. "I never saw this match coming. I didn't even though Dominic and Dazielle were dating."

"Um... it's a long story," I said.

"I heard there was another angel in the running for Dazielle's hand, but Dominic made his move, and she picked him," Auntie Queenie said.

"Something like that," I muttered.

"Sometimes, love just hits you right between the eyes and you can't help yourself. And Dominic is a looker," Granny Dottie said. "I wouldn't mind a squeeze with that one if I was available."

"Which you're not, old girl." Grandpa Lucius planted a big kiss on her red glossy lips.

"A whirlwind relationship is so romantic." Auntie Queenie leaned over and kissed Uncle Kenny's cheek. "This reminds me of our wedding. Although there were a lot fewer feathers and fewer ice sculptures."

He nodded as he took hold of her hand and kissed the back of it. "I remember it well. You were up on the tables with your skirt around your thighs, high kicking and sparking magic everywhere. It was an incredible sight."

"It doesn't look like Dazielle wants to do much dancing," Auntie Queenie said. "I've barely seen her crack a smile since she sat down. And she hasn't touched her food."

"She must be nervous about the wedding night. Or she's worried Dominic will be a disappointment in bed," Granny Dottie said with a snort of laughter.

"Dazielle's probably overwhelmed by it all," my mom said. "It's a big day. I always thought she was such an independent angel and would never tie the knot with anyone."

"Career women need love, too," Granny Dottie said. "And Dominic is a sweetheart. As dumb as a plank but pretty to look at. Dazielle is the brains, and he's the honey. It's a good combination."

"Dominic's a good guy," I said. "He doesn't deserve this."

"You don't think he should have married Dazielle?" Auntie Queenie's sharp gaze speared into me.

"Oh! No, that's not what I meant. It's just that he's not a showy guy. He probably doesn't like all this attention. Dazielle's mom is a bit of a social climber and expects great things from this marriage. I just hope Dominic can keep up."

"I've heard all about Hester," Granny Dottie said, her nose wrinkling. "She's done a few devious things to get where she wants to be."

"Do tell," Auntie Queenie said. "I love a bit of angel scandal. They always pretend they're so pure, but scratch beneath the feathers and you usually find lice."

"Later! The band's finished setting up. Let's be the first to hit the dance floor." Granny Dottie staggered to her feet, her cheeks flushed from all the champagne. She grabbed Grandpa Lucius's hand and waved the others to join her.

My mom leaned over to me. "Is everything okay? You've been quiet since the wedding ceremony. You're not really worried about Dominic, are you? I know you two are friends."

"He's got a few things to work out, but I'm sure they'll be okay." I looked at my empty glass. "I could do with another drink. Does anyone else want one?"

No one raised a hand, so I headed to the free bar with Wiggles trotting along beside me, snuffling up snacks and bits of food people had dropped. This place was greedy hellhound heaven.

I leaned against the bar and pinched the bridge of my nose. I needed to find a solution to this accidental marriage. There must be a get-out-of-marriage free card Dominic could use or a way to make sure their marriage wasn't legal for any longer than it needed to be.

"What would you like?" the bartender asked.

"Something that'll erase my memories of the last two days."

He grinned. "That bad, huh?"

"On the scale of awesome to earth shatteringly bad, I'm at the earth shatteringly bad stage. And it's all my fault."

He poured me something that smelt so strong it made my eyes water. "This will do the trick. Have fun."

"I'll have one of those," a deep, slightly slurred male voice said.

A strong smell of spicy cologne filled my nose, and I glanced up to see Gadreel, the former fiancé, standing beside me. "I know you."

He glanced down at me, his eyes bleary. "We haven't met."

"Not officially, but I'm friends with Dazielle. I'm... sorry things didn't work out between you two."

He lifted one shoulder and slugged back the shot the bartender had placed in front of him. He shuddered and tapped the empty glass. "I'll have another one of those."

"No hard feelings about not getting down the aisle to marry Dazielle?"

He grunted and drank the next shot.

I pursed my lips. "I guess not, since you've stuck around for the reception."

"It's a free bar. My free bar. Or, at least, it was supposed to be."

"You're not cut up about missing out on Dazielle?"

Gadreel stifled a burp behind his hand. "She's not worth thinking about. It's her loss."

My gaze drifted over Gadreel. He was handsome, but there was a coldness about him, and he had lousy manners. "I can see that."

He grinned at me before he threw back his third shot, staggering slightly as he thumped down the glass. "There are plenty more influential angels who won't want to miss out on me. I'll be married before the year is over."

"That sounds so romantic."

He chuckled too loudly and swayed some more. "I'm a catch. Everyone knows it. Dazielle has lost her mind. And who's the guy she's with? I've never heard of him. And I've been asking around. He doesn't even have a job. And I think he's younger than her."

"They're all terrible qualities to have," I said.

Gadreel smirked. "You and Dazielle are friends? How did that happen? She's usually not a fan of witches. She says they're always up to something."

"Oh, she's right. Never trust a witch. We're devious."

Gadreel glanced at the dance floor. "There are a lot of you here. Witch magic always tastes like burnt sugar to me. And you're powerful." His gaze moved up to my forehead. "Some of you more than others."

I brushed my hair over my forehead to conceal the angel mark. "I'm sure you'll wish Dominic and Dazielle well in their marriage. It's nice to see them so happy."

He tipped back his head and laughed. "You call that happy? Dazielle looks like she's been slapped around the face. She knows she's made a mistake. I expect she realized it when she saw me watching her take her vows. It hit her what a huge error she was making, but she couldn't back out. I don't know how she convinced her parents this was the right thing to do."

I smiled brightly. "I can't imagine how she did it."

Gadreel leaned closer, the alcohol on his breath drifting across my face and making me want to gag. "You're not bad looking for a witch."

"You're too kind."

"Are you single? Do you want to dance with the catch of the day?" He jiggled his hips from side to side. "You can tell me all about that angel mark on your forehead. You must have influence with the guys up top."

I lifted my hands. "I'm not single, I don't dance, and I don't know what you're talking about."

"Don't be so uptight." Gadreel grabbed my arm. "This is a wedding. People are supposed to enjoy themselves."

Wiggles looked up from his investigation of a lump of something green on the floor. He bared his teeth, and his eyes glowed as he advanced on Gadreel. "Back off, angel."

Gadreel dropped his hold on me and scurried away, almost knocking into a crowd of wedding guests. "I was only being friendly. There's no need to set that thing on me."

"Wiggles does exactly what he wants. He's also an excellent judge of character, and he clearly hates you. That means I do, too."

"Crazy witch." Gadreel turned and staggered away.

I looked down at Wiggles and shook my head. "Dazielle dodged a bullet there. He's about as charming as a squashed toad." I downed the shot the barkeeper had given me. My eyes watered, my chest burned, and a wonderful relaxing glow spread out from my chest, down to the tips of my fingers and toes. I let out a sigh as my worries vanished.

"There you are!" Granny Dottie boogied over and grabbed hold of my hands. "You're not getting out of dancing. Come with me."

I grinned as I followed Granny Dottie back to the dance floor and joined the large circle of family members.

"Is Aurora not joining us?" I said.

Granny Dottie shook her head. "I don't know what's wrong with that girl. I went to see her in the store earlier today, and she barely said two words to me. She kept sighing and staring out the window. I asked what was wrong, but she said nothing was the matter."

"I think I know what's wrong. I overheard her arguing with Zandra just before the wedding. She wasn't happy that I'd taken Zandra out on a demon hunt. But Aurora hates being around demons. I've asked her to come along a few times, but she always turned me down."

Granny Dottie clouted me on the back of my head.

"What was that for?"

"Daft girl! You're the reason they're fighting. I should have realized something was going on."

"They were fighting about me? Have I done something wrong?"

"No, but they look up to you. They both want to be your favorite."

"My favorite what?"

"Favorite sister."

"Can't they both be my favorite? Do I have to choose one over the other?"

"Of course not. But make sure they both know you care for them equally."

I frowned. "I feel like this is all my fault, yet I've done nothing wrong."

Granny Dottie arched an eyebrow. "You have been spending a lot of time with Zandra. Aurora is allowed to be jealous about that."

"But Zandra's taking time to adjust. I'm keeping an eye on her to make sure she's got a handle on her magic. You know she's been struggling."

"And we've all been offering her help, but she's a stubborn one. And she only seems to trust you."

"I'm not sure she does," I said. "How can I fix this? I don't want them fighting over me. Can't we just all get along?"

"They'll sort things out soon enough. Maybe those girls simply need to duke it out."

"You think I should let them fight? Zandra's magic is unpredictable. I don't want Aurora getting hurt."

"Aurora has power when she lets loose. She just keeps it close to her chest. Don't underestimate your sweet little sister. She comes from a powerful line of witches. If Zandra oversteps the boundaries with Aurora, she'll soon let her know."

"I should talk to them," I said. "I don't want them to have a magical showdown in the center of the village. Not over something so pointless."

"It's not pointless to them. Give them time to work things out, but if it gets tricky, you can always intervene."

"Tempest, we need to talk."

I froze on the spot then turned on my heel. Dazielle stood in front of me. She wore a stunning floor length white gown, and a long wedding veil trailed behind her, sparkling with hundreds of tiny crystals.

"Don't you look beautiful," Granny Dottie said. "You make such a lovely bride."

Dazielle inclined her head. "Thank you. Tempest, you're with me."

"I'm just having a dance with my family. I'll catch up with you later." I tried to catch hold of Granny Dottie's hand, but she was already dancing away.

"Now. This can't wait." Dazielle caught my arm in a vice-like grip and dragged me off the dance floor.

Dominic was waiting by the edge of the dance floor and cast me an apologetic look as he walked along beside us.

"The food was great," I said lamely. "And Granny Dottie loves the champagne. If she has any more, she'll float from all the bubbles."

Dazielle grunted and muttered something under her breath. She shoved open a door and pushed me through before gesturing Dominic in. Wiggles snuck through the door just before it shut.

"Was this a big game for you?" Dazielle crossed her arms over her chest and glowered at me. "We needed your help to make sure the marriage didn't happen, and you sat back and watched it go ahead.

Were you laughing at us while we were forced to say our vows?"

I squeezed my eyes shut for a second. "I had every intention of stopping the wedding."

"Then what went wrong?"

"Sorry about this, Tempest," Dominic said.

"No, you're not apologizing for anything," Dazielle snapped. "Tempest owes us an explanation."

"I do. Sorry, I shouldn't have said I do. It must bring back bad memories of earlier today."

"Explain yourself," Dazielle growled out. "And do it quickly, or I'll have you arrested."

"What for?"

"Breaking a promise."

"Then you need to be arrested, too. And I'll add blackmail to your charges."

"That's why you messed this up? Payback?"

"No! And I really didn't mean for things to go wrong."

"We'd just like to know how we ended up married angels," Dominic said.

The look on his face was so sad, I stopped arguing. "I was waiting at the back of the chapel, when I heard my sisters fighting. I went to break them up, and by the time I got back, it was too late. Dominic was kissing you."

"Your sisters were fighting?" Dazielle ground out from between her teeth. "Unless it was a fight to the death, you should have left them to it."

"Dazielle doesn't mean that," Dominic said. "Family is important."

"I do mean it," Dazielle said. "We have to undo this."

"And I'll help you do that," I said.

Dazielle shook her head. "We've seen exactly where your help gets us. I'm married to a---"

"Sweet, funny angel who tries to make everyone smile. It could be worse."

"Thanks, Tempest. We'll make the best of it," Dominic said. "And everyone has been so generous with their gifts. There's a whole room full of them."

"Forget the gifts! There's nothing to make out of this fake marriage," Dazielle said. She glared at me for several tense seconds. "Since Tempest has offered to help, I have a plan to fix things."

"Let's hear it," I said. "I figured there must be a way out of this marriage. Some loophole in the vows or something like that?"

"There is a way out. You're going to claim you had an affair with Dominic. Then I can annul our pairing."

My mouth dropped open. "I'm not being painted as the scarlet witch in this situation."

"You just said you'd help. This would help."

"I'd look like a marriage wrecker. I'm not doing that. If a guy is coupled up, he's off-limits. I don't go after other women's men."

"But you couldn't resist Dominic," Dazielle said. "You fell for his charms and seduced him."

"No! And still no!"

"It's believable. Everyone knows Dominic is sweet on you," Dazielle said.

His cheeks flushed. "They do?"

"No, they don't," I said.

"They totally do," Wiggles said.

"It's the perfect solution. When you realized I was taking him as my husband, you made a move. In his drunken state at the wedding, Dominic slipped up. You ended up in bed together, and—"

"No! I will not be labeled a marriage wrecker. There has to be another way. Can't you just say you made a mistake?"

"After everything I did to convince my mom we were in love? She'd hang me out to dry if I backed out of this relationship. I can't change my mind again."

"How about you stay married for a year? After that, you could say things didn't work out, and you're more friends than lovers."

"It would ruin the family reputation. Once an angel is married, that's it. Relationship breakdowns are frowned upon."

"But you're okay for me to pull your marriage apart by saying I cheated with Dominic?"

"That's different."

"It isn't different," Dominic said. "And my mom would be devastated if she thought I'd done that. Not that I would. I'm never unfaithful to the woman I love."

"I think I can smell a hog roast." Wiggles trotted to the external door and sniffed along it. "Is there an evening buffet?"

"No," Dazielle said on an exasperated sigh. "And Mom would never order a hog roast. She says they're uncouth, and everything gets greasy from the pig fat."

"Mmmmm, pig fat. I definitely smell something," Wiggles said. "It smells amazing."

Dazielle tutted at him before glaring back at me. "I could force you to do this. Don't think I won't bring Zandra in for questioning."

"You've already used that piece of blackmail on me. It won't work again. Now I know you're looking at Zandra, I'll make sure she's being extra careful to keep out of your way."

She sighed and yanked off her veil before tossing it to the floor. "This is a sham marriage. I'm a sham!"

"I need some air." Dominic stuffed his hands in his pockets and walked away.

"Now look what you've done. You've upset Dominic," I said.

"I don't care about him."

"You should, since he's your new husband." I backed away as Dazielle advanced on me, her wings swiping through the air.

"Don't try my patience, witch. You've messed with me one too many times."

"Relax! Take a leaf out of Dominic's book and go clear your head. There'll be a solution to this, but it's not me faking an affair with your new husband."

Dazielle scrubbed her fingers through her carefully pinned curls, knocking several loose. "I just... I didn't expect this to happen."

"Get some air, take a break from all the crazy marriage stuff, and then we'll come back to this problem. And I will help you. I didn't plan for this to mess up so badly."

She glowered at me before turning and stamping away.

A member of the catering staff walked past with a huge tray of wedding cake. I grabbed several plates and then leaned against the wall and closed my eyes.

A hard nose nudged my leg.

I opened my eyes and set a plate down for Wiggles. "You wanted some angel food cake. Here it is."

He sniffed the air again. "I'm more interested in the roasting meat. It's got me drooling."

"Eat the cake." I stuffed a huge piece in my mouth. "Did you see where Dominic went?"

"Out the side door. I've never seen the guy look so down. Although I'd look miserable if I just got married to the grumpiest bride in the world."

I ate more cake as I leaned my head back against the wall. "There has to be a workaround to get those two free from each other."

"Give them time. I bet Dazielle will eventually fall for Dominic's clumsy charm. He's a decent angel. One of the better ones."

"You're much more optimistic than me about this relationship." I ate all the cake, not caring that it made me feel sick because of all the super sweet pink icing.

I lingered in the room for as long as I could, ignoring the curious looks from the caterers as they dashed back and forth from the kitchen with tray loads of treats to serve the wedding party.

I couldn't put this off much longer. I had to return to the party and face Dazielle's continued death stares.

Dominic crashed through the external door, his chest heaving. He rushed over and grabbed my hand.

"Dominic! What's the matter?"

He looked over his shoulder. "I've just found a body in the garden."

Chapter 6

Dominic kept a tight hold of my hand as we stared down at the body of an angel. She lay on her front, her short blonde hair messed up. There were burn marks on her back, and her wings were gone, dumped in a pile beside her.

"Do you know who it is?" I said.

"I think it's Dazielle's friend, Irin."

"This is what I could smell," Wiggles said. "Look at the marks on her back." He was trotting around the body, sniffing the air.

Dominic gagged. "Who would cut off her wings and then leave them? You sometimes hear of evil supernaturals trying to take angel wings because of the power the feathers hold, but it's senseless to do this."

I looked away from the scorched flesh and the nubs on Irin's back that were all that remained of her once magnificent wings. I knelt and checked her pulse, almost relieved when I didn't find one. An angel with no wings was an oddity, and Irin would have been lost without her feathers.

"Let's move away from her. We don't want to contaminate any evidence," I said. "And this murder looks recent. The killer won't be far away."

Dominic quickly backed away, his hand still squeezing mine. "This has to be the work of another angel. Very few supernaturals can destroy one of us."

"That doesn't narrow it down much," Wiggles said. "There are hundreds of angels in the other room."

"Not all of them would have known Irin," I said.

"What shall we tell people? This is my wedding party. Should I ask people to leave? Won't there be panic when they learn someone has been killed?"

The door leading out into the small private garden banged open.

Hester hurried out, a radiant picture of shimmering white. "Dominic! Where's Dazielle? I haven't seen her for a while, and the guests are asking about her."

I stood in front of the body. "She's not out here. Go back inside, Hester."

"Why? What's going on out here?" Hester peered around me. She blinked several times then staggered back a step. "Is that an angel?"

"Dominic, take Hester inside," I said. "She doesn't need to see this."

"Please don't tell me that's Dazielle." Hester's hand shot to her chest.

"No! It's not Dazielle. We think it's one of her friends, though."

"An angel is dead?" Hester swayed from side to side before collapsing into Dominic's arms.

He held her up then looked at me. "What shall I do with her?"

I had to keep control of this situation before word got out about the murder, and I had a garden full of panicked, drunk supernaturals to deal with.

"Get Hester out of here. Carry her inside and make sure she's somewhere quiet. Wait with her until she wakes up. She'll most likely panic, so you need to keep her as calm and quiet as possible. The second she screams murder, we'll be out of time."

Without a second of hesitation, Dominic lifted Hester into his arms as if she weighed nothing more than a bag of sugar and strode away.

"Wiggles, go get Mom, Uncle Kenny, and Grandpa Lucius. I need them out here so we can deal with any crowd that wants to take a look. Get everyone else to send the guests home. Tell them what happened to Irin, but make sure the guests don't overhear. If people ask questions, tell them there's been an accident and someone's been hurt. And make sure people know they have to stay in the village until the morning. I don't want anyone sneaking out of Willow Tree Falls until they've been discounted from this murder investigation."

"I'm on it." Wiggles bounded away.

I glanced back at the dead angel. I wanted to cover her body, but I couldn't risk disturbing any evidence.

I turned back to the reception venue. The entire local branch of Angel Force had turned out to celebrate Dominic and Dazielle's wedding, and I needed to get them out here and following my orders. Not all the angels who worked with Dazielle were as obliging as Dominic. Some even made it clear they resented a witch being involved in their work.

My fingers drifted to my forehead, and I rubbed it. It was time to try out this higher angel mark. This mark meant something to the angels, and I needed to see how much power I could wield with it.

I closed my eyes, rested my palm against my forehead, and exhaled slowly. I imagined contacting all the angels who worked with Dazielle and summoning them out here.

Within thirty seconds, the door was opening, and angels were hurrying toward me. At the front was Cassiel, and she looked mad as anything.

"How did you do that?" she snapped. "I just got your command in my head and had no option but to follow it. Did you use magic on me?"

"I used this." I pointed at my forehead. "And it was out of necessity. There's been a murder." I stepped aside so everyone could get a look at the scene behind me.

The angels gathered around Cassiel, several of them looking as annoyed as she did.

Her jaw clenched as she looked at the angel on the ground, her expression morphing into shock. "Who is it?"

"I haven't turned her over, but I think it's Irin. And I need your help. Dominic just discovered the body, and the murder's not long happened. I'm pretty sure the killer could still be around."

There were murmurs from the crowd of angels.

"I need everyone to listen to me. We have to secure this scene, examine the body, and then get to work on finding out who did this."

"You're not our boss," Cassiel said.

"No, but your boss is about to have her wedding day ruined. She doesn't know about this yet, but she soon will. We have to look after things for her. I don't expect you to like me giving the orders, but I do expect your cooperation." I tapped the mark on my forehead. "Does everyone understand me?"

There were several unhappy grumbles, but they all nodded.

I looked around the group for a friendly face. I spotted lots of tense expressions but then saw Jophiel and Oriel, who stood to one side of the group. It was rare to see Oriel out of the Angel Force office.

"Jophiel, you're with me. Cassiel, do an on-site examination of the body and then remove it with Oriel's help. I need everyone else to look around, see if there are any clues as to who did this and any sign of an escape route. And be careful. There's a supernatural out there who can bring down an angel."

No one moved.

I pulled back my shoulders. "It must be horrible that someone you know has been killed like this, but we have to keep this professional. Get searching and report back to me with anything you find."

The angels moved away. Cassiel peered at the body, while Oriel hovered beside her.

The next to arrive were Mom, Grandpa Lucius, and Uncle Kenny.

I hurried over to them. "Has Wiggles told you what's happened?"

"Yes. An angel's dead," Mom said. "Is it anyone we know?"

"No, it's a friend of Dazielle's. I need you here to keep people calm. The guests will want to know what's happening, and they might come to take a look."

"They're already asking questions," Mom said. "Don't worry. Granny Dottie's taken control. They won't mess with her when she orders them to leave."

"I've got the angels searching the scene, so don't touch anything. Just look out for anyone coming to take a sneaky look around."

"Of course. We'll handle that. You focus on helping this poor angel." Mom gave me a quick hug. "How are you? Did you find the body?"

"I'm fine. I mean, it's never fun seeing a body. Dominic actually found her."

Mom gave me another hug. "Does Dazielle know yet?"

"Not yet. I'm dreading telling her. I'm not sure how close they were."

"She can't be left in the dark about this." She touched my cheek. "Do you want me to tell her?"

"Thanks! Yes, that would be helpful. You're always so good at keeping people calm, and I shouldn't leave the scene."

"I'll break it to her gently." Mom gripped my hand tight. "What are you going to do?"

"I'm going to figure out who murdered this angel and make them pay."

Chapter 7

Two hours of sleep, six mugs of strong coffee, and dozens of concerned wedding guests spoken to, and I was done in.

Tilly placed another mug on the table in front of me and squeezed my shoulder. "Rough night?"

I nodded. I'd temporarily retreated to her restaurant to get some quiet and mull over everything I'd found out. "It's not one I want to repeat. Handling angels is like herding giant, overexcited cats. They want attention all the time."

"Drink that. It'll help."

I pushed the mug away. "Thanks, but if I have another coffee, I'll be climbing up the walls."

"Which is why that's hot chocolate," Tilly said, "with extra cream and sprinkles."

Wiggles' head appeared from under the table where he'd been snoozing on my feet. "Are you making waffles? All this detective work makes me hungry."

"You've been asleep for hours, not sleuthing. I had to carry you here because you were too tired to walk."

"I'm stress eating for both of us," he said.

"I don't usually open for breakfast," Tilly said. "And you need to keep your nose out of sight. I'm not supposed to have animals in the restaurant."

"No one else is here," Wiggles said. "Please, can we have waffles? I think better on a full stomach."

My stomach grumbled at the thought of Tilly's delicious, fluffy waffles dripping in syrup.

Tilly chuckled. "I'll heat the waffle maker."

"Don't make them just for him. Wiggles has plenty of reserves to live off."

"I'm not. You're getting some too, and so am I." Tilly headed behind the counter and assembled the waffle ingredients. "They should be ready in about ten minutes."

I lifted my mug and took a sip of the delicious hot chocolate. "I'd love to hide out here all day, but we'd better take them to go. I need to head to Angel Force to see if they found anything useful on the body. Cassiel should have finished her examination by now."

Tilly shook her head as she whipped batter. "I'm still amazed how anyone killed an angel and no one noticed. She must have put up a fight."

"I didn't see any bruising or marks on her body, but then Irin was face down on the ground, so I didn't get a great look at her."

"And no one you spoke to last night heard sounds of fighting or an argument?"

"No. And the music was on, so that would have drowned out any noise from the garden."

"Who have you got left to speak to?" Tilly asked.

"I've ruled out almost everyone. There were quite a few people at the wedding who didn't even know

Irin. Those who did have alibis. They were sitting at a table with other guests or on the dance floor. I'm left with a handful of people who knew Irin and had a connection to her."

Tilly arched an eyebrow. "Does that include Dazielle?"

I nodded. "She was in shock last night. I spoke to her briefly, then everything got hectic with interviewing wedding guests and handling the angels. And they're not that keen on taking orders from me."

"They need someone to handle things. It can't be Dazielle."

"She wasn't fit for doing anything other than staring into space, so I've temporarily taken over until they find someone else to step in."

Tilly grinned. "I imagine some of them grumbled about that."

"It was rude grumbling. I didn't know angels knew so many cuss words."

"How's Dominic doing? He must have had a double shock yesterday, getting married to Dazielle and then finding a body." The smell of sweet waffles filled the air.

"I imagine he won't want to relive that night anytime soon."

Tilly tilted her head. "I still can't believe they got married. Did you know they were seeing each other? Was it a secret office romance that got serious? I always thought Dominic irritated Dazielle."

I hated keeping things from Tilly, but the fewer people who knew about the sham marriage, the better. "Sometimes, these things just happen."

Tilly pursed her lips, clearly not believing my brushoff. "Is that so?"

I lifted my mug and studied the contents.

She huffed out a breath. "I know not to prod when you're working a case. You sit there and enjoy your hot chocolate. I'll make up an extra-large order of waffles to go."

"Thanks, Tilly. You're the best."

Wiggles rested his chin on my knee. "You don't think Dazielle was involved in this murder, do you? I mean, she can be grumpy, but is she a killer?"

"A few people I spoke to said Irin and Dazielle had a tense relationship, but I can't imagine Dazielle wanting the memory of murdering someone on her wedding day lodged in her head."

"It was a unique wedding. Maybe she gave herself a unique gift."

I scooped some cream off the top of my hot chocolate and let Wiggles lick it off my finger. "She's innocent. And hopefully, now she's thought about things, she'll be more useful today. I don't want to be in charge of her angels any longer than I have to be."

I had my own business to deal with, and I couldn't neglect that for too long. Although I had a great team around me who looked after the place while I was busy.

Five minutes later, and with a delicious smelling bag in my hand, I left the restaurant with Wiggles, and we walked to Angel Force.

It was still early, but the streets were busy with angels wandering around and peering into the stores. It looked like they'd listened to my advice not to leave the village.

We walked through the doors at Angel Force and through the reception into the back office.

Several angels working at their desks looked up at me and nodded.

I headed over to Cassiel, who was perched on the edge of a desk, sipping a drink.

She eyed me up and down as I stopped in front of her. "Yes?"

"Good morning, sunshine. Shall we talk murder?"

Cassiel's frowned deepened. She sighed and gestured for me to follow her.

"Did you get anything useful off Irin's body?" I set down the bag of waffles and strolled after her.

"Nothing clear that points us to who did it," she said. "Do you want to take a look?"

"Not really. I wouldn't know what to look for."

"Dazielle always does when she's in charge of an investigation." Cassiel glanced at me, and her top lip curled up.

"I don't want you to think I'm shirking my duties. Let's go take a quick look." We headed into the medical room.

Cassiel stopped by the door and pointed at Wiggles. "You stay here."

Smoke billowed out of his mouth. "Where Tempest goes, I go."

"You'll mess around with things. I don't trust you." Cassiel shooed him away.

Wiggles looked up at me and lifted a paw.

"I'll be two minutes. Stand guard."

His eyes glowed red, and he growled at Cassiel before turning his back on her.

Cassiel led me into the room then uncovered Irin's body.

"I don't see any obvious signs of a fight." I looked at her hands and arms and took a quick peek at her face.

"There are no bruising or cuts, other than the obvious damage to the wings."

"And that's what killed her? Would an angel losing her wings be a death sentence?"

"Not necessarily. If she'd gotten treatment quickly, she could have survived. It was most likely the shock that killed her."

I looked over at the pile of feathers sitting on an adjacent table. "What does a wingless angel do with her life?"

"Not much. There are a few communes that take them in and try to give them a purpose. Our wings are a big part of our identity. They're connected to our essence and power. An angel without her wings is an aberration, and no one knows how to treat her." Cassiel shook her head. "Wingless angels tend not to live for long. It was probably a good thing Irin died. She wouldn't have had much of a life."

I glanced back at the door. "Just before we found the body, Wiggles smelled burning flesh. He thought it was a hog roast. Was something hot used to cut off Irin's wings?"

"Your hound has a good nose. I can't say for certain, because the murder weapon hasn't been found, but the wings were sliced off cleanly. I'll turn her over and show you what I mean."

My gut clenched, and I gritted my teeth as Cassiel moved the body. This was why I could never do this work full-time. I didn't have the stomach for the gory bits.

"Come closer. She won't bite," Cassiel said.

I shuffled nearer. "The cuts on the wings look clean, as if something sharp went through them only once. Were the feathers burned?"

"Correct on both counts. It would have needed to be something wicked sharp to slice off an angel wing in a single blow. Sharp and extra hot. Whatever was used slashed through some skin as well, so there are burn marks on the body."

"It must have been a big knife to get through the wings in one go."

"Most likely."

"And whoever used it must have been strong."

"And fast. The killer would have had to sneak up on Irin without her hearing. That's why there are no signs of a struggle. She didn't get a chance to defend herself."

"Maybe Irin knew her killer," I said. "She didn't think she was in danger, so she turned her back on whoever struck her."

"That's also possible," Cassiel said. "How many suspects are we looking at?"

"There are five people I'd like to talk to again," I said. "Everyone else has been discounted. They either have alibis or no connection to Irin."

Cassiel's expression hardened. "Dazielle had better not be on that list."

I took a step back. "She might be. Will that be a problem? This case needs to be handled impartially."

"Dazielle wouldn't do this. She's a great boss. We don't want anyone else running this place."

"I'm not here to cause trouble for Dazielle."

"But you're in charge? Why does it have to be you?"

"It doesn't. I'll speak to Dazielle this morning, figure something out, and we'll go from there. Believe me, I don't want to be in charge any longer than I need to be."

"Good. Because a witch in charge of angels is too odd."

"You'll hear no arguments from me."

Cassiel jabbed a finger at me. "And I know you had something to do with why Dazielle married Dominic. She kept muttering your name and cursing during the wedding dinner. What did you do to force them to get married?"

I lifted my hands. "I didn't force them, but maybe things didn't go to plan on the day." That was another thing on my to-do list. I had to find a solution to get Dazielle and Dominic unmarried.

Cassiel grunted and flipped the cover back over the body. "I just don't want things to change around here." She continued grumbling under her breath, but her back was turned to me, so I guessed that meant the conversation was over.

I left the room and headed back into the office with Wiggles.

"Did you find out anything useful?" he asked.

"Not really. There were no fight marks, and whatever cut off her wings was big, sharp, and hot. Oh, and Cassiel hates me."

Wiggles snorted out smoke. "Some things never change."

When I got back to the office, the bag with my waffles in it was missing. I looked around and saw several angels busily munching.

I gritted my teeth. So that's how it was going to be. I'd keep a careful grip on my snacks the next time I came in.

I opened the door to Dazielle's office to find Hester inside.

She stepped away from the desk and snapped her purse shut. "Tempest! What are you doing barging in here?"

I glanced at the desk Hester had been investigating and then at her purse. "I'm looking for Dazielle. What are you doing here?"

"Nothing! The same as you, actually. I'm looking for my daughter." Hester clutched her purse. "I'm worried about her."

"Everyone is. Do you know if she got much sleep? It was late when I saw her, and she seemed a bit confused."

"I insisted she go home, so I know she got a little sleep. Dazielle kept saying she needed to work, but I assured her you were overseeing things. Although that didn't help calm her. It just made her tense up and pace around."

I tried not to smile. Dazielle would hate that I was in charge.

There was a tap on the door, and I turned to see the wedding officiant, Lailah, standing outside. She wore a pristine white pants suit with a flouncy blouse.

She gave me a quick smile. "Sorry to interrupt, but I have an important message for you, Tempest."

"Don't mind me. I should get going anyway," Hester said.

"I thought you were waiting for Dazielle?" I said.

"I can't wait for my daughter all day. Perhaps she didn't feel up to coming into the office. I'll go see if she's in her apartment." Hester scurried out, her purse still clasped in her hand.

I doubted she'd be there. Dazielle wouldn't be having a lie-in when a friend had just been murdered. And I was surprised not to see her here, barking orders at the angels and ushering in suspects to quiz.

I looked back at the desk. What had Hester been up to in here? I moved toward it and took a look on the surface. As usual, it was neat and tidy, no files were where they shouldn't be, and all the important paperwork was tucked away.

Lailah cleared her throat. "I don't like to press you, but the message is from the higher angels. They were most insistent they see you as soon as possible."

"Oh! They've heard about Irin's murder?"

Lailah nodded. "They're concerned. They've asked that I bring you to them right away."

"You can do that?"

She nodded. "Just hold my hand. I'll take us right there."

I looked around Dazielle's office one more time. There was nothing obvious missing, so it didn't look like Hester had taken anything. And why would she want to steal from her daughter, anyway?

I walked over to Lailah and took her hand. "Wiggles, you wait here."

"Fine by me. I need to talk to some angels about my missing waffles."

I nodded at Lailah. "Let's go see what the higher angels make of this murder."

The world tilted as Lailah's angel magic enveloped me, and we disappeared.

Chapter 8

My stomach flipped like I'd just been on a giant rollercoaster. We arrived in a large white chamber with a covering of mist on the floor.

Lailah gave my hand a reassuring squeeze before letting go. "Don't worry. They're very friendly."

"I've met three of them before. How many higher angels are there?"

Her eyes widened a fraction as she glanced at my forehead. "Not that many. Not anymore." She stepped back and bowed her head.

Two glowing angels materialized out of thin air. It was Liliana and Emmeline. I'd met them months ago when working on a case.

Liliana nodded at me. Her features were indistinct because a glow radiated from her skin, but I recognized her straight away. "Welcome back, Tempest. It pleased us to learn you're helping our angels during this troubling time."

"Hey, Liliana."

Lailah squeaked and shook her head at me.

"Is something wrong?" I asked.

"No! I mean... you don't usually address them by their names."

"Oh, okay. What should I call them? Your royal glowiness?"

"All is well, but thank you for noticing, Lailah. Tempest does not know our ways, so we make allowances for her," Liliana said.

"You won't smite me for messing up on the rule following?" I said.

Liliana's smile was benevolent. "Not today. We have already reached our smiting quota."

"That's good to know. A dead witch isn't usually a helpful one."

"We could re-animate you, but you might not be so cooperative," Emmeline said.

"I'd agree with that. If you killed me, we'd never be friends." I glanced at Lailah, but her head was down, and she was shaking.

Liliana pressed a hand to Emmeline's arm. "Tell us of your progress with the murder investigation, Tempest."

"I'm doing what I can to figure out what happened to Irin. Do you know anything about the victim that could be useful?"

"We do." Liliana flapped out a large silk handkerchief and dabbed her eyes. "She was a valuable asset. We have all shed tears over her loss."

"I'm sorry to hear that. Was she in the running for higher angel status?"

"No, nothing like that, but she was a future thinker. She had plans." Liliana tucked away the handkerchief. "We will offer you what knowledge we have to help you find the killer."

"I'd appreciate that. We have already eliminated most of the guests who attended the wedding. I worked with a team of angels through the night to speak to as many of them as possible. I'm now focusing on those closest to the victim."

Emmeline hovered closer. "Does that include Dazielle?"

I narrowed my eyes a fraction, not liking the intense look in her dazzling blue eyes. "It does, but only as a technicality. I understand you can't think she'd be involved with this murder."

The angels looked at each other for a minute, as if they were communicating without speaking.

"Or am I missing something?" I said. "I don't do telepathy, so you'll have to fill me in using that magical thing we call language."

Liliana turned back to me. "It's only right you know everything, to make sure you can complete a fair investigation."

"Oh! I wasn't planning on running this whole investigation. I figured Dazielle wouldn't lead on it, but you'd find someone else or bring in another team of angels who weren't so close to the victim."

"We believe it's best that Dazielle isn't involved at all." Liliana's smile made me dizzy. "Tempest, we want you to lead this investigation."

I shook my head. "The other angels won't think much of that. I'm just a temporary stand-in. Cassiel could take over. She's always methodical with the bodies. She'd be thorough."

"Cassiel is a fine angel, but her skills aren't with people. And she can be a little... sharp."

I grinned. "That's one way of describing her rudeness. But surely someone else would be better to lead this. Someone who won't annoy the investigating angels."

"We insist you do it," Emmeline said. "And we're temporarily suspending Dazielle from duty, so she can't be a negative influence."

"Is that necessary? Couldn't you just put her on another case?" I tapped a finger against my chin. "And she is due a honeymoon."

The angels shared another long look again.

I sighed. "You're doing that mind talking thing again. You need to keep me in the loop. What's going on? Why are you shutting out Dazielle?"

"Irin and Dazielle had... a difficult relationship," Liliana said.

"A few of the wedding guests said a similar thing. What made it difficult?"

"They served on several committees over the years and even went through the same college together. They used to be close friends."

"But something changed? I figured they were still close since Irin was at the wedding."

"Ah... the wedding. I'd almost forgotten. That's another puzzle to come back to." Liliana's huge wings flared out. "Irin was an astonishing angel. The miracles she created hadn't been seen for generations. She also had huge ambitions to revolutionize the work conducted by Angel Force."

"And Dazielle was unhappy with those ambitions?"

Liliana nodded. "They had a number of public disagreements. We've recorded several of them in committee meeting minutes. I shall send them to you."

"So they had a few arguments. Why would Dazielle want to kill Irin on her wedding day?"

"We don't know for sure that she did, but they had an ongoing feud that was causing concern. We'd spoken to both of them about their disagreement, and they assured us everything was in hand."

"You don't think Dazielle was jealous of Irin's success, do you? You said she was an up-and-coming angel."

"They worked in different industries, so I don't think there was a professional jealousy at work," Liliana said. "Irin worked in mergers and acquisitions. She was looking into privatizing the services Angel Force provides."

My eyebrows shot up. "Irin wanted to create a private police force to handle crime?"

"Not so much the crime solving, but she had developed a persuasive argument to show we could save resources by outsourcing some of the current work of Angel Force. Dealing with fines, crowd control, peace keeping, that sort of thing."

"I imagine Dazielle thought little of that. She's not big on changing things."

"That was the source of their disagreement. Irin had been working on this plan for two years. She presented us with her final report and recommendations less than a month ago. We've been considering the plans and were excited by her proposals. We could see the benefits."

"Dazielle not so much?"

"Unfortunately, Dazielle hasn't been a fan of any of Irin's suggestions. We received a separate report from her, refuting Irin's proposals and outlining the problems with it. Her main concern was the lack of professionalism when things become privately outsourced. Companies would bid to undercut each other, which could degrade the service quality and potentially give Angel Force a bad reputation."

"That sounds like a valid point," I said. "You usually get what you pay for. But I'm still not convinced Dazielle would kill Irin over this. After all, Irin's done the work and given you her proposal. You can implement everything she suggested, even though she's dead."

Liliana shook her head. "Irin set up a company specifically to provide these resources. She was the chief executive."

I choked out a laugh. "Our victim gave you a proposal to outsource Angel Force services and just happened to head up an organization that would provide them. Isn't that a massive conflict of interest?"

The higher angels shared another look.

"Irin wouldn't have directly supplied the services. Her company would only have overseen the proposals submitted to run them," Emmeline said.

"And I imagine Irin would have received a big commission or fee for doing so?"

Liliana's brow furrowed. "I... yes. I believe so."

My nose wrinkled. That seemed dodgy to me. No wonder Dazielle wasn't impressed with Irin's plans.

Liliana clasped her hands together. "It will take a long time to find another angel with Irin's vision to carry out these plans."

I sucked in a deep breath as a jolt of worry hit me. "You're thinking Dazielle got desperate? She sent in a report that detailed why Irin's proposals shouldn't go ahead, but it sounds like you favored the plans to privatize things. Does Dazielle know about this?"

Liliana's image shimmered, and the surrounding air cooled. "She does. She wasn't happy when she found out."

"And you're worried Dazielle took Irin out of the equation to stall the project and give herself time to convince you it was the wrong direction to go."

The higher angels shared another long look. I didn't need to be a mind reader to see the concern on their faces.

Liliana turned back to me. "It was a concern of ours. Which is why we need you to lead this investigation. Dazielle is too close to this for a number of reasons, one of them being her long association with the victim. We believe she must be considered the prime suspect."

"I wouldn't say prime suspect. And I haven't had a chance to check her alibi. She could have been with someone when Irin was killed." I thought back to the previous night. I might have been the last one to see Dazielle before the murder happened. We'd been arguing about the mess up with the wedding, and then she'd stormed off. I hadn't seen her after that. I'd been busy stuffing my face with delicious cake. But Dazielle must have gone back to the wedding reception. Someone would have seen her.

"Do we have your word you'll investigate for us?" Liliana said. "We need this handled discreetly and quickly. Both Dazielle and Irin had important reputations."

Although Dazielle could be a royal pain in my backside, I owed her big time after accidentally getting her married to Dominic.

I nodded. "I'll do what I can to figure out what happened at the wedding."

"Very good. I knew we could rely on you." Liliana glanced at Lailah. "Might I suggest you work with Lailah? She's a reliable angel and excellent in her job as a ceremony officiant. She's also well-known in the community and liked by all. She'd make you an excellent assistant."

Lailah nodded. "Thank you. I'm discreet, and I've developed a talent for blending in at events. It's easy to do when people are there to celebrate and party. I could be useful and might even overhear something that would help solve this murder."

I preferred to work alone, but Lailah could be handy to have around. "I've got no problem with having an assistant." A friendly angel working alongside me could smooth things over and maybe even make the other angels less resistant to me being in charge.

"Then it's agreed. You'll return to Willow Tree Falls so you can get on the case right away," Liliana said.

Emmeline nodded as the angels slowly vanished from sight.

I turned to Lailah. "Are you okay with helping? I guess when the higher angels tell you to do something, you have little choice but to obey."

"I'm happy to help. I liked Irin, and I know Dazielle. And Dominic seems like a lovely angel. It's a tragedy this happened on their big day."

"Yep. It wasn't the best timing."

Lailah wobbled her head from side to side. "Although neither of them seemed happy when I married them. I was concerned they might have been having second thoughts but didn't like to change their minds at the last second. And then there was the sudden change of groom Hester insisted upon. It all left me rather confused."

"You're not the only one."

"Dazielle mentioned she'd worked with Dominic for a long time, and it's not uncommon for relationships to develop in the workplace. I've seen many happy unions from couples who've met through work. I'm sure Dazielle and Dominic will be blissfully happy." She extended her hand to me. "Shall we get investigating?"

I caught hold of her hand and nodded. "Take me home."

The world tilted again, and we arrived outside Dazielle's office.

Hester rushed up to me, her bottom lip wobbling and her eyes filled with tears.

"Hester! Is something wrong with Dazielle?"

She shook her head and pulled back her shoulders. "No. But I have a confession to make. I murdered Irin."

Chapter 9

Wiggles bounded over as I stared in shock at Hester. "This crazy angel has been running around demanding to see you."

I gave him a quick pet on the head. "Thanks, Wiggles. Hester, let's go into Dazielle's office. We can talk in private in there."

Hester glanced around then nodded. "Very well. But I need to tell you what happened. I can't hide what I did any longer."

Lailah and Wiggles came into the office with Hester and me.

I shut the door, took a deep breath, and turned to her. "Take a seat."

She perched on the edge of a chair, her back straight. "What happens now?"

I looked at Dazielle's large, empty chair. It felt wrong to sit in it, but it also felt sort of right. Dazielle coveted this chair and never let anyone else use it.

I walked over, eased myself into her chair, and sighed. It was so warm and comfortable. No wonder Dazielle didn't want anyone else to sit in it.

"Tempest!" Hester snapped. "I just confessed to Irin's murder. You need to arrest me."

I leaned forward. "Let's go back to the beginning."

The office door burst open, and Dazielle rushed through, panting for breath, her cheeks pale. "Mom! Don't do it."

Hester glanced at her daughter. "It's too late. I've already told Tempest the truth."

Dazielle rushed over and grabbed her mom's arm. "You didn't kill Irin."

I hurried over and shut the door again to make sure the curious angels outside couldn't listen in to this weird conversation. "Dazielle, calm down. I was just about to ask your mom some questions."

"How can I be calm?" She stared at me, desperation and confusion in her tired eyes. "I don't know why Mom's doing this, but she's lying to you."

"We'll have none of that lying talk. Angels don't deceive people."

"But you didn't do it," Dazielle said. "Why would you kill Irin? This makes no sense."

"I have my reasons," Hester said. "And I want my confession formally recorded by Tempest. I did it. You don't need to look for anyone else."

Dazielle stared at me, a pleading expression on her face. "Don't arrest my mom for this murder. It'll be a mistake."

I lifted a hand as I returned to Dazielle's seat. The fact she didn't protest told me just how stressed she was. "Let's sort through this before anyone goes making confessions or arrests."

"There's nothing to sort," Hester said. "I won't have this murder on my conscience a moment longer."

"Before we talk murder, let me fill you both in on what's been going on. Lailah and I have been to visit the higher angels. They've asked that I lead on this investigation."

Dazielle glared at me for a second then nodded. "Of course. It would be hard to find any of my angels who are impartial."

"I wasn't all that keen, but they insisted."

Dazielle grunted. "Do they really think you're the best person for the job?"

I snorted a laugh. "I'm pretty sure I'm not, but they were convinced I had to do it. And Lailah's assisting me. They said it would help to have an angel on side during the interviews."

Dazielle looked at Lailah. "I have no problems with you being involved."

"I'll do the best I can to help you, Dazielle," Lailah said. "This all seems like a horrible muddle. We'll make things right." She glanced at Hester.

I also studied Hester. Her confession to the murder made no sense. "Okay, since I'm in charge, I need a couple of important things before I begin. First, I need breakfast. Your angels ate what I brought in earlier."

Dazielle pursed her lips then sighed. "Your hellhound has stolen plenty of their food over the years. Call it payback."

"I borrowed it," Wiggles said. "With no intention of giving it back."

"And I don't think clearly when I'm running on empty," I said. "I need fuel."

"Very well. I'll send someone out for breakfast," Dazielle said. "What else?"

"I need a private space so I can interview Hester. And Dazielle, you can't be involved in the interview. You're too close to this."

"She's my mom! I want to represent her."

"I can represent myself." Hester patted Dazielle's hand. "You should go home and rest."

"I can't rest. You're about to be charged with a murder you didn't do."

"You see! You can't interview your mom. You'll do anything to show she's innocent. I'll get all the facts and keep you informed, but I can't risk you influencing her," I said.

Dazielle scowled at me. "I wouldn't do that."

"I would if my mom was up on a murder charge," I said. "I'd do everything I could, legal and illegal, to stop her from going to jail."

She lowered her head. "Don't push her into a confession. Get all the information first before making a move."

I nodded. That was fair, and it was exactly what I'd planned to do.

The office door creaked open, and Dominic looked around the side. "I got a message saying I needed to get to the office. Is everything okay?"

"Not really," I said. "You'd better get in here."

"You have a bride who needs comforting," Wiggles said.

Dominic's cheeks flushed as he hurried in and closed the door. "What can I do to help?"

"Nothing, unless you can make my mom see sense," Dazielle said.

Dominic's eyes widened. He walked over and wrapped a stiff arm around Dazielle's shoulders. "What's wrong with... Mom?"

Hester shook her head. "You two shouldn't even be here. Go off and enjoy your honeymoon. Don't worry about me."

"There won't be a honeymoon," Dazielle said.

"There is. It's all paid for," Hester said. "Two weeks in Sunny Sands. It's warm, private, and romantic."

"That sounds nice," Dominic said.

Dazielle glared at him and shrugged his arm off her shoulders. "We're not going on vacation while my mom just confessed to Irin's murder."

His mouth dropped open, and he stared at Hester. "You killed Irin?"

"No! And I'm trying to figure out why she's lying about it," Dazielle said.

"Dominic, take Dazielle out of here. Go get her a coffee or maybe something stronger. She's had a shock."

"I'm not leaving Mom," Dazielle said.

"I need to interview her. And Lailah will be with me, so it'll be above board. We need to figure this out, but I can't do that while you're here."

Dominic hovered by Dazielle and Hester, seeming unsure what to do.

I caught hold of his elbow and tugged him out of the office. "Dominic, I need your head in the game. Dazielle is in the way, and I have to figure out why Hester just confessed to this murder. Plus, we still have other suspects to look at. None of this makes sense, so I need you on my side with this. You need to be useful."

He ran a hand down his face then nodded. "Sorry. I just keep getting shock after shock at the moment. I'm still recovering from marrying my ex-boss. Although the honeymoon does sound fun. Maybe I should suggest we go on that. It would keep Dazielle out of your way."

"Only if you want Dazielle to choke you to death."

"Oh! Yes, right. That was a bad idea."

I stepped closer and lowered my voice. "I have to ask this since you found the body, but what were you doing just before that? We were talking with Dazielle, and then you walked away."

He did an owl-like blink. "You don't think I had anything to do with it?"

"I'm only asking to eliminate you."

"Oh, of course. I... I went to the washroom and splashed water on my face. There were several other wedding guests in there. I can give you their names. Then I went outside to grab a breath of air, and that's when I found Irin. To begin with, I thought it was a guest who'd had too much to drink, but there was this awful smell in the air, and then I saw the wings. I ran straight back to get you."

I took a note of the names of the people who'd seen him. "Thanks. I don't think you did it, but I have to cover all the bases. Now, you need to get Dazielle out of here. She's freaking out because of what her mom confessed to doing."

"Why would Hester kill Irin?"

"That's what I need to find out. Please, go deal with your bride."

He grimaced. "I'll never get used to Dazielle being my wife."

"Hopefully, you won't have to for long. I promise, I haven't forgotten I dropped you in it by getting you married to Dazielle. I will make things right."

"Of course. I trust you." Dominic pulled back his shoulders. "Right. Into battle I go." He marched into the office. After a minute of conversation with Dazielle, she skulked out in front of him, looking furious.

She glared at me. "Don't be too hard on my mom."

"I only want to get to the truth." I walked back into the office and closed the door. Lailah was in a seat, and Wiggles had somehow convinced her it was a good idea for him to sit on her lap. She was stroking his head, and he had his eyes closed.

"We might as well do the interview in here," I said. "If you're okay with that, Hester?"

"That's fine. I just want to get this over with," she said.

I looked over at Lailah, and she nodded at me. I sat back in Dazielle's seat. "Hester, at this stage in the investigation, I'm just collecting basic information."

"Why? I've already confessed. Arrest me, charge me, and close the case."

"Not so fast. I understand you've confessed, but I need details before we go any further."

She clasped her hands around her knees. "What do you need to know?"

"How did you know Irin?"

"Anyone with an interest in making the right connections knew Irin. She had the ear of the higher angels, and if she didn't know a particular person, that was because they weren't worth knowing."

"You got to know her because of her connections?"

"We moved in the same circles. And she went to school with Dazielle. I knew her when she was much younger. I always thought she was a smart young woman, who would go places."

"Talk me through your movements at the wedding reception," I said.

Irritation flashed across Hester's face. "It's not necessary. I killed Irin. I can't say it any other way."

"I still need the facts. I know the basics. We were all at the ceremony, then the photographs were taken. What did you do after that?"

"The same as you. We went in and had a sit down meal. I was on the top table with Dazielle and Dominic."

I nodded. It had been impossible to miss Hester as she presided over events. She outshone her daughter with her natural glow and flowing hair.

"Then what?"

"The music started. That's when the tables broke up."

"What did you do after that?"

"I mingled for a while, and then I killed Irin."

"Where did you kill her?"

Hester glanced at me and looked away. "In the garden."

"And how did you kill her?"

She licked her lips. "I cut off her wings."

"What did you use?"

"Something sharp."

"If I might interrupt," Lailah said, "a normal blade won't cut through an angel's wings. They're too tough."

"It would need to be infused with magic?" I said.

"Possibly," Lailah said.

"Everyone knows that," Hester said. "And I'm a powerful angel. If I want to remove another angel's wings, then that's what I'll do. I'm perfectly capable." She shuddered in her seat.

"What did you do with the murder weapon?" I said.

"It's gone. You'll never find it."

"I'd like to try. If I can find the sharp object... did you say it was a knife?"

Hester tucked her wings into place. "I didn't. You don't need any more information from me."

"If I can locate the murder weapon, it will add weight to your confession."

"My word should be enough. Everyone trusts me."

"Yet I'm not convinced you're being honest," I said. "You killed Irin, somehow disposed of this mysterious weapon, returned to the wedding party, and then put on a great act when you discovered us with Irin's body. Your reaction seemed genuine when you saw her on the ground. You fainted into Dominic's arms."

Hester didn't respond.

I looked over at Lailah, whose eyes were a little wide as she watched Hester. She caught my eye and shrugged.

"Let's assume you killed Irin. Why do that?"

Hester was silent for a few seconds. "Irin was ambitious, and Dazielle had spoken about her worries for the future of Angel Force. I couldn't bear the thought of seeing my daughter unemployed. Imagine what people would think! So I saw an opportunity to remove the problem."

"You killed Irin so Dazielle wouldn't lose her job?"

"I had to protect Dazielle. That's what a mother does."

I glanced at Lailah, who lifted her shoulders again. Wiggles was now slumped across her knees, snoring softly.

"What were you doing in here when I arrived this morning?"

"You already know the answer to that question. I was waiting for Dazielle."

"It looked to me like you were poking around."

"Is it a crime to have an interest in your child's job?"

"It depends. Were you looking for something specific?"

"No. Just a piece of paper and a pen to write a note to Dazielle."

"There was no note on the desk when you left."

"That's because you interrupted me. I forgot to leave one." Hester shifted in her seat again.

"Let's move on to Dazielle," I said. "You mentioned she was concerned about Irin's work. And I've spoken to the higher angels. They confirmed there were several disagreements between Dazielle and Irin."

"Oh! They are aware of that? Well, Dazielle is always a professional, but she stands her ground when she has to. If she was disagreeing with Irin, it would have been valid, but they'd have worked things out."

"Dazielle has more motive for killing Irin than you do. If Irin's plan to overhaul Angel Force takes place, it would mean a huge upheaval. And we both know Dazielle isn't a fan of change."

"You have a point. But you're forgetting one crucial thing," Hester said. "Dazielle was the bride. All eyes were on her for the entire day. How could someone under such scrutiny have gotten away with murder?"

Lailah leaned forward in her seat. "I saw Dazielle not long before the murder took place. She went out a side door of the venue. I didn't see where she went, though. Maybe she found a way to sneak out and be on her own."

Hester glared at Lailah. "That's not relevant. Even if Dazielle was on her own for a few minutes, she wouldn't have had time to kill Hester. And she was wearing a huge white wedding dress. Surely there'd have been blood on the dress if she'd been involved. And what did she do with the murder weapon? She could hardly slip it down her corset."

They were all valid points, but I still wasn't convinced Hester was the killer.

"Let's get this dealt with." Hester glanced over her shoulder. "Perhaps I should have an angel charge me, since you don't seem capable."

"I'm more than capable of slapping your feathery behind in a cell, but I'm not charging you with anything at the moment."

"This is outrageous."

"So is lying about killing someone."

"I'm not lying!"

I leaned forward and fixed Hester with a glare. "I will hold you in a cell while we do follow-up interviews with the remaining suspects."

"There are no other suspects. Are you some kind of idiot?"

"I wasn't the last time I checked, but things change." I stood, opened the door, and called two other angels in. "Put Hester in a cell. Make sure she's comfortable."

Hester glowered at me. "I'll ensure the higher angels hear of your incompetence. You'll be banned from working with the angels."

"Be my guest. They're following this case with interest." I watched as Hester was led away to the cells. Then I shut the door and turned to Lailah. "What do you think?"

She shook her head. "I think we should talk to those other suspects."

"You're not convinced Hester killed Irin?"

"No. I've known that family a long time, and I'm the same age as Dazielle and Irin. We were in college together. And I don't like to speak badly about anyone, but Dazielle's mom is a massive social climber."

"I figured that out for myself. Why is that important?"

"Because she'd never do anything to sully her reputation. Committing murder is out of the question. She'd be too terrified of being found out and having everything taken away from her."

"So why is Hester so readily confessing to Irin's murder? Her reputation will be ruined if this charge sticks."

Lailah tugged on her bottom lip. "She doesn't want someone else to take the blame?"

"That's what I think, too. We need to get out there and do some digging. An angel is lying, and we need to find out who it is."

Chapter 10

"Who shall we question next?" Lailah walked beside me as we headed out of the office, Wiggles trotting along between us.

"Dazielle is the obvious target. If Hester's protecting anyone, it'll be her daughter. And she said it herself, she needs to safeguard Dazielle's career."

Two angels dashed past us and raced out the door.

"They're in a hurry. What's going on?" Lailah said.

"I have no idea. Let's go find out." I hurried after the angels with Lailah and Wiggles.

They were faster than us as they took flight, but they were headed straight into the village. I broke into a jog and chased after them.

As I caught up with the angels, I was shocked to see Aurora and Zandra with their arms wrapped around each other, and they weren't having a friendly hug. Something pink and white was squashed between them.

The angels hovered around them, their wings outstretched as sparks of magic flew off my sisters.

"Leave this to me," I ordered the angels as I raced over.

They backed away a few steps, concern on their faces as magic continued to flicker in the air.

"We had reports of a fight," one of them said. "We didn't realize it was your sisters. Are you sure you don't need any help?"

"Thanks, but I've got it from here." I grabbed Zandra's arm and yelped, leaping away as a painful spark shot up my arm.

I tried to get hold of Aurora, grabbing her around the waist and pulling her back, but my nose filled with an itching sensation, and I let go as I was overcome with a sneezing fit.

"Are you okay?" Lailah patted my back. "Who are they?"

"Aurora and Zandra, my two terrible sisters." I coughed out the last of Aurora's magic and stood upright. "You two, quit fighting, or I'll let Frank loose and he can deal with you."

Aurora glanced at me. I took a step back, surprised by the anger blazing in her eyes.

"Aurora, calm down. This doesn't help Frank. You know how he gets when you're overexcited."

"I'm not excited, but I am going to make this witch pay."

I glanced at the two angels who were still hovering. They looked like they were about to arrest my sisters at any second. "Lailah, can you do me a favor? Go take those angels for a cup of coffee. I don't want this to get out of hand."

"Are you certain you can handle them? I feel the energy coming off them. Those witches are powerful."

"They're Crypt witches. They're supposed to be powerful. We'll be fine. I just don't want anyone to get arrested or injured."

"I'll come with you," Wiggles said. "I'll show you the best places to eat around here. And you can treat me to a couple of muffins as a thank you."

"No chocolate," I said to him.

"Nope. I'm in the mood for cream caramel or maybe salted peanut butter and fudge muffins. Follow me, Lailah."

Lailah and Wiggles headed over to the angels, and after a short conversation, they walked away.

Now I had no distractions, I turned my full attention to my squabbling sisters. I sparked a knock back spell, took careful aim, and blasted it in between them.

They shot apart and landed on their backs in the dirt. A sad looking bouquet with a long string of white ribbon wound around it fell to the ground.

I stood in between them, magic sparking on the ends of my fingers. "What's going on?"

Aurora was the first to scramble to her feet. She brushed dirt off her clothes and glared at me. "Zandra stole something from me."

"No, I didn't. It was mine. I caught it." Zandra got to her feet.

"Caught what?" I said.

"Dazielle's bouquet at the wedding," Aurora said.

"I didn't see either of you at the wedding. How come you got the bouquet?"

"I came, but I didn't stay long," Aurora said. "I wasn't in the mood for a party. I dropped by to see Dazielle and Dominic as they came out of the chapel and had their pictures taken. After the photographs, Dazielle threw her bouquet."

I'd missed that bit after wandering off to take a breather from all the hyped up wedding guests. "Okay, but I'm still confused. You're fighting over flowers?"

"We caught the bouquet at the same time," Zandra said.

"No! My hand got there first, then you yanked away the flowers," Aurora said. "It's mine."

"You were too slow. Your fingers might have brushed it mid-air, but I got a good hold on it. Therefore, it's mine."

Aurora stamped her foot, and magic sparked along the ground.

"Calm down," I said. "Who cares about a bouquet of flowers?"

"They were so beautiful," Aurora said. "I planned to press some and give them to Dazielle and Dominic in a frame so they have a nice memory of their happy day together."

"I planned to press them and be an annoying sappy witch. Yuck! You're such a good girl. Always doing things to make other people happy," Zandra said in a mocking tone.

"Unlike you, who goes out of your way to be mean. And you smirk at everyone like you're trying to win the Queen of the Smug Jerk Contest. You get pleasure out of making other people miserable."

"It makes me happy to see you miserable," Zandra said.

I stared at each sister. They really seemed to hate each other. Then I recalled Granny Dottie's words. Were they doing this because they wanted my attention?

"There's no need to fight over flowers," I said. "How about we figure this out over dinner?"

"I'm not eating with her," Zandra said.

"And I don't want to eat with you. You probably only eat hotdogs or things from a tin."

"What's wrong with hotdogs?"

"Stop! Aurora, you're already married so you don't need the bouquet."

"But... but I was going to make a gift for—"

"That's not important. Dominic and Dazielle already have enough gifts. And Zandra, do you even like flowers?"

She shrugged. "I'm not bothered either way."

"And do you want to get married? Isn't there some old wives' tale about the person who catches the bouquet will be the next to get married? Is that why you're so possessive over the flowers? You're looking to get hitched?"

Zandra grimaced. "No way! I'm never letting a guy tie me down."

"Marriage doesn't tie you down. It liberates you," Aurora said. "I've never been happier."

Zandra made a rude noise in the back of her throat. "You're so annoying."

Lailah walked back toward us with two takeout mugs in her hands. The other two angels were nowhere to be seen, but Wiggles was by her side, wagging his tail and happily munching.

I grabbed the bouquet off the ground and presented it to him. "There you go. Wiggles can have it. Problem solved."

"What am I supposed to do with those?" He looked up at me.

"Just take them. I'll explain later."

Wiggles finished chewing and grabbed the bouquet between his teeth.

"She still shouldn't have stolen from me," Aurora said.

"And you shouldn't tell lies and make out like I'm a thief." Zandra took a step toward Aurora.

I sighed. Maybe the problem wasn't solved, after all. I pressed a hand against my forehead. "I'm done with you two. There are bigger problems I have to concentrate on. You can sort out your differences like mature witches. And if you can't figure out how to do that, don't expect me to come to your funerals."

Aurora looked shamefaced and lowered her hand, which had been pointed at Zandra and sparking with a magic spell. "I heard about the murder. Are you investigating?"

"I have no choice. The higher angels put me in charge."

Zandra tilted her head. "They're the head honchos who oversee angel business?"

"Something like that. And I've got a mess on my hands trying to find out who killed Irin. I have to focus on that, not your argument. Can you sort this out or not?"

"Sorry. We'll figure things out," Aurora said, but the glare she shot Zandra was anything but friendly.

"There's nothing to sort out. I'm not looking to be a part of Aurora's life," Zandra said. "I just had to set her right over the stealing accusation."

"You need to get used to being a part of Aurora's life. We're in the same family."

Zandra grumbled under her breath but didn't agree with me.

"Dad won't want to see you fighting with each other. I can't help you right now, but how about dinner tonight?"

They both nodded grudgingly.

"I vote for pizza," Zandra said.

"Of course you would," Aurora said. "I want sushi."

"Well, you can't have slimy fish wrapped in gross green stuff that smells of the sea."

"It's seaweed, idiot. And I can eat what I like. Besides, sushi doesn't give you spots. It's good for you."

"You still can't have it. They don't serve sushi in Mystic Mushroom. And that's where we're going for dinner," Zandra said.

"I can eat whatever I like. And I don't want to share a greasy pizza with you."

"I would never share my pizza with you."

I groaned and tipped back my head.

"It seems your sisters have a few issues to sort out," Lailah whispered as she handed me a large takeout mug.

I took the top off and had a big sip. It was hot chocolate. "This is a new situation. They're struggling to adjust."

"Have they always been like this with each other?"

"Nope. Zandra's a recent addition to the family."

"Oh! Adopted?"

"No. Complicated."

Lailah nodded and sipped her drink.

I hopped in between Aurora and Zandra before they came to blows again. "How about Tilly's restaurant? She serves everything. She does Artisan pizza, sushi, whatever you like."

"Tilly's is expensive," Zandra said.

"I'm paying for dinner, so you can't use that as an excuse," I said.

"I guess it doesn't sound so terrible. Can we have three courses?"

"Eat whatever you like. Just be there."

"It's a great choice," Aurora said. "I'm definitely coming."

"Perfect. Just don't bring your boxing gloves. We need to talk over your problems and sort them out."

"Yeah, yeah. Whatever you say, big sis," Zandra said.

Aurora glanced over at her store. "I have to get back to work. I'll see you tonight? Seven o'clock?"

"Yep, that works for me," I said. "Zandra?"

"Sure. Whatever." She turned and stalked away.

Aurora looked longingly at the bouquet in Wiggles' mouth.

"Don't even think about taking that thing," I said. "It's dirty and covered in dog drool."

She sighed. "I was only trying to do a good thing. And I caught it first. Zandra only lunged for the bouquet when she saw I was about to get it."

I arched an eyebrow at her. "Don't you have customers waiting?"

Aurora looked like she wanted to argue some more but then turned and dashed away into her store.

Wiggles spat out the bouquet. "I'll put in an order for steak with Tilly. She never lets me inside the restaurant when it's busy, so she must get everything ready for me outside."

"I'm sure Tilly will be happy to serve you steak." I watched Aurora as she bustled around her store.

"Try not to worry about your sisters," Lailah said. "Families are always complicated. I've got six siblings, and we always fight when we get together. It's not that we don't love each other, but sometimes, we drive each other mad because we're so different. Three of them work for Angel Force, and they always tease me about my job."

"Teasing is in a sibling's job description." I rolled my shoulders. "I could do with a break after that. Although we really should go deal with Dazielle."

"We can take half an hour," Lailah said. "And if it helps, I'll tell you everything I know about Irin if you think it could be useful to the investigation."

I smiled at her. "Anything you have on Irin could be helpful. And thanks for the hot chocolate. Since Dazielle never got around to sorting out our breakfast, let's go grab some food and see if we can't figure out this murder between us."

Chapter 11

I settled on a bench outside Sprinkles with Lailah. We'd grabbed a small box of donuts and had them open between us.

Wiggles sat by my feet, looking ever hopeful as I munched on a caramel cream donut with chocolate sprinkles. The big hit of calories and energy was just what I needed after dealing with my feisty sisters.

"So, you knew Irin and Dazielle in college?" I asked Lailah.

"We took some of the same classes. We weren't best friends, but we'd hang out together sometimes. We'd often see each other at parties and that kind of thing. I could always tell Irin would go places. You know when you meet someone and they dazzle you? She was so switched on and always did things at double the speed of anyone else. Irin was a go-getter from a young age."

"Do you know much about Irin's business ambitions?"

"A little. And I know they weren't popular with some people."

"Including Dazielle?"

Lailah nodded. She pulled off a piece of donut and fed it to Wiggles. "I officiate all kinds of ceremonies for the angels. Weddings are my biggest business, but I do funerals, cleansing ceremonies, vow renewals, you name it. I'm happy to do it. When you go to these kinds of events, there is often plenty to drink, and people like to talk. Over the last year or so, I've heard discussions about the privatization plan."

"I imagine those working for Angel Force have their concerns."

"Some of them hate it, especially the ones who've always done things a certain way."

"And Dazielle's been running Angel Force around here for a long time." I glanced at Lailah. "Do you have an opinion about Irin's modernization plans?"

She chewed on her piece of donut and swallowed. "I don't like to think of anyone losing their job, but the measures Irin had planned would mean some angels could be out of work."

"Who would get their jobs? Or would they just be phased out?"

"From what I understand, other supernaturals would take over. And that was the real rub for many. Angel Force has always been run by the angels."

"With a name like that, it's no surprise," Wiggles said.

Lailah petted his head. "And I don't like to blow my celestial trumpet, but angels are the pinnacle of supernatural creatures. We're strong, fast, smart, and not unattractive to look at." She grinned. "But seriously, we've always had the job of law enforcement because we're fair and practical. We always ask questions first and assume innocence until proven guilty. Could you imagine how law enforcement would operate if the werewolves were in charge? Or the gremlins?"

"I've been around the local branch of Angel Force for a while, and not all the angels who work there are that efficient. Some of them can even be sneaky. Maybe a shakeup is what they need."

Lailah pursed her lips. "You could be right. Sometimes, people get so used to doing something a particular way that they don't want to question if it's the best way, or the fastest way, or even the cheapest way. I know that was a concern of Dazielle's."

"The cost issue?"

"Yes. She doesn't want services to be driven by how cheaply they could be run, because it would impact quality."

"I see how that would make Dazielle angry," I said. "But I've worked with her for a while, and she's no killer. Although... this isn't the first time she's been accused of murder."

Lailah's eyes widened. "Really? I've not heard that before. What happened?"

"It's a long story. And she was innocent. I just can't see her killing Irin. Hester made some valid points about how Dazielle could not commit this murder unseen."

"I agree. But I haven't been close to Dazielle for a while. You know what it's like; people lose touch as they get older. Maybe she's changed."

"I doubt she's changed that much." I finished my hot chocolate. "What did you think about Hester's confession?"

"I can't see her as the killer," Lailah said. "As I said, Hester has a certain position within angel social circles. She highly values that position."

"I get that, but I also get she's a mom, and moms are protective of their kids. I know if I was ever in trouble, my mom would defend me with her very last breath, even if I was in the wrong."

Lailah reached for another donut. "Hester hasn't always been supportive of Dazielle's choices. And although Dazielle never complained about her, well not much, I don't think she was always happy at home. Her mom ruled her life. Which is why I was so surprised at the last minute change of groom. Gadreel and Dazielle have always been destined to marry each other."

"It's a weird one." I stared ahead. It didn't seem right to hide the fake love story from Lailah, not when she was being so helpful.

"And I'd never heard of Dominic until Hester announced Dazielle was to marry him. He seemed like such a surprising match for her."

"Um... there is more to that story than you know," I said. "Can you keep a secret?"

Lailah set down her donut. "I keep hundreds of secrets. Some of the confessions brides and grooms tell me just before they get married would turn your hair white. My lips are always sealed. It's one of the key roles of being an officiant."

"You can't tell anyone else."

"You have my word."

I glanced around to make sure no one was listening. "Dazielle couldn't face marrying Gadreel. She hates him, and I've never seen her so panicked before. The marriage would have been terrible for her."

Lailah was quiet for a few seconds. "I don't know Gadreel well, but I met him a few times before the ceremony. For an angel, he's charmless. He even made a lewd suggestion to me during a meeting to discuss the ceremony. I laughed it off and acted like I didn't understand him, but I could tell he was being serious."

"I haven't had much to do with Gadreel, but he was unpleasant when I spoke to him at the wedding reception. Dazielle couldn't face being with a guy who wouldn't treat her right, so we came up with a plan. Dazielle decided to convince her mom she was in love with another angel, so her wedding to Gadreel would be canceled."

Lailah gasped. "But instead, Hester insisted Dazielle marry Dominic?"

"You got it."

"Dazielle and Dominic aren't really in love?"

"No, and they just about tolerate each other. But they have worked together for years, so they know each other well."

Lailah licked sugar off her fingers. "I've just married two angels in a sham wedding?"

"By mistake. The wedding wasn't even meant to happen. I was supposed to stop the ceremony."

"But you didn't. What went wrong?"

"I was planning to interrupt at the appropriate moment, but I missed my cue. You've just met the squabbling reason that happened. I got distracted by my sisters, and by the time I got back, it was too late."

Lailah ate a piece of donut, a smile spreading across her face. Then she chuckled. The chuckle grew into full-blown laughter. She wrapped her arm around her middle and kept laughing.

"It's not funny! I'm involved in this mess." I started laughing, too.

Lailah wiped a tear from the corner of her eye as she continued to chuckle. "I'm so sorry, but it's like a comedy of errors. Oh, forgive me for laughing. I do feel sorry for Dazielle. And no wonder Dominic looked so downcast when I declared they were married. I thought he was about to cry. Some grooms do tear up on their big day, but his face suggested it was the end of the world. Now, I know why."

I sat back on the bench, relieved to have revealed the secret. "I feel awful for messing up. Is there any way you can pretend the marriage never happened? Lose the certificate or something?"

"I wish it was that simple, but no, they're officially married. But there are ways to end an unsuitable marriage. Although I'm not sure what Hester will think about that. Angels tend not to separate once they're joined. There could be a scandal."

"She'll have to put up with the scandal. We need to un-marry them as soon as we've figured out who killed Irin." I finished my donut and licked caramel cream off my fingers. Now I was fortified with food, I felt ready to deal with Dazielle. "Let's go do that interview I've been putting off."

"Do you think Dazielle will mind being questioned?" Lailah collected the remains of our food, gave Wiggles her last bite of donut, and then put the rest in the trash.

"She won't be happy, but I doubt she'll be surprised. And she'll want to know what's going on with her mom, so it's unlikely she'll get mean."

"I don't have experience interviewing people. I hope I don't make a mess of things."

"You must interview couples who are about to get married," I said.

"Oh, I suppose I do. I like to think of them more as informal chats. It's a way to get to know the happy couple and see how strong their connection is."

"Did you ever talk to Dazielle and Gadreel together?"

She shook her head. "I only ever spoke to them separately. Dazielle was always so busy looking after Angel Force, so I understood why she didn't have time to meet up with Gadreel. Although now I see she was probably avoiding him, rather than being too busy. She really disliked him that much?"

We left the bench and headed to Dazielle's apartment. "Most likely. Do you know what Gadreel does for work?"

"He worked for Irin. And I think the job earns him a decent amount, because he always wears tailored suits."

"He's a handsome angel, but I didn't get a good vibe from him at the wedding. He's on my list of suspects to quiz, but let's deal with Dazielle first."

We entered Dazielle's apartment building, and I knocked on the door.

She yanked it open. "What's going on? Have you released my mom yet?"

"Not yet. And we're keeping her in the cells, since she's confessed to the murder."

Dazielle glanced out the door and then ushered us in. She led us into her living room. "You know she didn't do it."

"Which is why I'm still asking questions," I said.

Wiggles wandered around and snuffled under the couch.

Dazielle let out a sigh and slumped onto the couch, shooing Wiggles away. "This is such a mess. First, my awful wedding—" She glanced at Lailah.

"I've told Lailah everything. And I mean everything."

"Even... Dominic?"

I nodded. "I didn't want to keep her in the dark, since she's helping with the interviews."

Dazielle hung her head. "I'm not proud of what I did, but I was desperate not to marry Gadreel. I might even have been tempted to marry Tempest if it gave me a way out."

"You're such a sweetheart," I said.

Lailah walked over and patted Dazielle's shoulder. "I understand. Marriage is a complicated business."

"Am I in trouble?"

Lailah smiled warmly. "Not with me. But we'll need to figure out a solution to your marriage problem."

"After we figure out who murdered Irin," I said.

Dazielle nudged Wiggles away from the couch.

"Wiggles, leave the nice couch alone," I said.

He dropped to his belly and tried to squeeze under the small gap between the floor and the couch. "There's something under here."

"Maybe you dropped some food, and it rolled under there?" I said to Dazielle. "Wiggles has a nose for treats."

"I don't abandon food on the floor." Dazielle grabbed Wiggles and held him out at arms' length. "Holy angels! You're heavy!"

He huffed out smoke as she returned him to me and placed him by my feet.

"Sit!" Dazielle pointed at Wiggles.

"Um... you have met Wiggles before, right? He doesn't do commands."

"I do when food is involved. And it isn't food I can smell under that couch."

Dazielle returned to her seat. "There's nothing under there. I clean weekly."

"Leave the couch alone," I muttered to him. "Go bother Lailah. She likes you."

Wiggles trotted over to Lailah, who was settled on the end of the couch, and presented his belly to be rubbed.

"Dazielle, I need to ask you some questions about Irin," I said.

She lifted her head. "I figured you would. Go on, what do you need to know?"

I sat in the seat opposite Dazielle. "I've heard from several sources that you and Irin had a difficult relationship. Tell me about that."

"It wasn't... well, we used to be good friends at college. Things went wrong when she set up her own company and began planning changes to Angel Force."

"What did you think of those changes?"

"Not much. At first, I figured she just wanted a debate on the subject. I never thought she'd send a proposal to the higher angels about ruining a structure that's been in place for thousands of years."

"What happened when you learned what she'd done?"

"I confronted her, but Irin dug her heels in. She said it was the right thing to do, and Angel Force was outdated and inefficient."

"And you were unhappy about that?"

Dazielle arched her eyebrows. "The idea of a mass privatization of Angel Force is ridiculous. It would never work."

"If you no longer considered her a friend, why was she at your wedding?" I said.

"I had no control over who came to the wedding," Dazielle said. "Mom arranged that. And Irin had influence and connections. That appealed to my mom. She wanted Irin there to show off how extravagant the wedding was."

"How far did your grievance with Irin go?"

Dazielle's nostrils expanded as she drew in a deep breath. "I'm not sure what you mean."

"I mean, did you hate her enough to kill her?"

"No! I just wanted her to change her mind and stop messing with Angel Force."

I kept an eye on Wiggles, who was inching across the floor on his belly. "And how far were you prepared to go to make sure she changed her mind?"

"Not as far as murder," Dazielle said. "I'd lodged a complaint with the higher angels and sent them my report showing why it was a terrible idea to privatize Angel Force. I was confident they'd see sense."

"They weren't seeing sense. I met with them, and they were interested in what Irin recommended. They said she was going places."

Dazielle shifted in her seat. "Perhaps they'll change their mind now she's gone."

"Your disagreement with Irin gives you a motive for killing her," I said.

She sighed. "I see that. But killing Irin wouldn't have solved the problems."

"It might have made you feel better."

"For about five seconds. But if the higher angels want to go ahead with her plans, it could still be done. My team would be pulled apart for the sake of saving money."

"Were you worried your career was at risk because of Irin's plans?"

Dazielle shook her head, but there was doubt in her eyes. "I would have found myself something else if the worst happened. I'm not sure what, but my experience and reputation wouldn't leave me out of work for long."

"You've always enjoyed working at Angel Force," Lailah said. "It would be hard to adjust to a different job."

"I was hoping it wouldn't come to that," Dazielle said.

"The higher angels mentioned you and Irin fought in several meetings," I said.

"No! Our conversations got a bit heated, but that's it."

"Did you ever threaten Irin?"

"I'm not an idiot. If I was planning on murdering someone, I'd keep my threats to myself and get on with the job when no one was paying any attention. And I definitely wouldn't do it on my wedding day."

Lailah jumped as a pile of papers appeared on her lap.

"Where did they come from?" I said.

Lailah touched the papers and smiled. "The higher angels. They have an unsettling habit of literally dropping things on me when they want my attention." She peered at the paperwork for a few seconds. "These are meeting minutes."

"Why have they sent you those?" I asked.

Lailah flicked through them, and her eyes widened. She glanced at Dazielle. "Tempest, you'd better look at this."

I took the papers from her. There was nothing interesting until I turned to the third page.

"Wiggles! Stop that," Dazielle said.

I looked up to see he'd wedged himself under the couch, his back legs kicking and his butt in the air.

"Tempest! Pull him out before he destroys the couch. He'll tear the fabric if he keeps wriggling about like that," Dazielle said.

"I'll do it." Lailah stood and knelt beside Wiggles. "What have you got under there that's so interesting?"

"He's a menace," Dazielle said.

"He's got something in his mouth." Lailah lifted Wiggles and cradled him like a baby. She eased her fingers into his mouth and pulled out a small felt mouse.

"Give that to me!" Dazielle snatched it away.

"It smells funny," Wiggles said.

"You don't have pets, Dazielle," I said.

She glanced at a closed door behind her. "I do now."

I grinned. "What have you got?"

"A kitten. Well, I thought she was just a kitten, but she's odd. I'm thinking about taking her back."

"Don't you dare! You took the kitten on, you have to keep her. Where is she?"

Dazielle glanced at the door again. "No idea."

I stood, strode to the door, and pulled it open. A ball of white fur and glittering magic rolled out. The kitten was so small she'd have easily fit into the palm of my hand.

She hissed at me and launched herself at my leg.

I easily dodged the angry furball. "Easy, puss. I mean you no harm. Wiggles, come take a look. She's so cute."

He was perched on the back of the couch, staring down at the kitten with huge eyes. "I'm fine here."

I laughed. "She's tiny. She won't... ouch!" The kitten grabbed my leg and sank her tiny teeth into me.

"You were saying?" Wiggles said.

Dazielle hurried over and eased the kitten off me. "See what I mean? I was looking for a quiet companion, not some demon in kitten's clothing."

I rubbed my leg. "What's her name?"

"Phantom."

Phantom leaped from Dazielle's arms. She froze when she spotted Wiggles, stood on her tiptoes, and puffed up so she looked like a fluffy shower loofah.

Wiggles ducked behind the couch cushions.

Phantom tried to jump up to get him, but she was too small to make such a mighty leap.

Dazielle helped her, and Phantom spiraled through the air and landed on Wiggles' back. She grabbed his ear in her mouth and growled.

"I really should take her back to the pet store." Dazielle sighed as Wiggles and Phantom tussled. "Especially with everything that's going on."

"A distraction is just what you need. Keep her." I returned to my seat and grabbed the papers. "You need something positive to focus on."

"What's in those meeting minutes?" Dazielle remained standing as the couch was taken over by Wiggles and Phantom's increasingly frantic tussling.

I looked up at Dazielle and saw concern in her eyes. There was no way to sugar coat this. "It states here that you made threats toward Irin."

"Not murder threats!" Dazielle said. "I... maybe I got hot-headed when we discussed her plans. She wouldn't see my side of the story. She kept saying her way was the only way. Irin was railroading the higher angels into these changes. I had to make sure they saw sense, and I needed to get her to drop her plans for privatization."

"And you thought threatening her would change her mind?"

Dazielle threw up her hands. "I was desperate. She wasn't listening to me."

I handed the paperwork back to Lailah. "Which again, gives you a reason for wanting her dead."

Dazielle was quiet for a moment as she watched Phantom get rolled over by Wiggles. "I suppose if I was investigating this case, I'd suspect me."

"What's your alibi?" I said. "You walked off after we talked. What did you do then?"

She closed her eyes. "I needed to be on my own. It was too overwhelming, going from getting out of my marriage to Gadreel to being accidentally married to Dominic. And my mom was so excited. She was showing off everything to the guests and telling them how much money she'd spent on making the day perfect. I needed a break. So I went for a walk in the grounds."

"Were you alone?"

"Yes. I felt like I couldn't get enough air in my lungs and was about to pass out. I walked around the gardens and then returned to the party. By then, Irin had just been discovered."

"You didn't see a single person when you were out there?"

Dazielle shook her head. "I heard a few voices but kept out of people's way. I couldn't force another fake smile and hear anyone else congratulate me. It all felt so false."

"Did you hear any arguing or the sounds of a fight? Irin's body was discovered close to the back entrance of the venue. Maybe you saw someone running away from that direction."

"I didn't hear or see anything unusual, but I was focused on my own problems. I wasn't paying much attention to anything else."

I glanced at Lailah, and she gave me a slight shrug. Dazielle had a strong motive, an opportunity, and she'd hidden the fact she'd threatened Irin. Was she really the killer and her mom was covering for her?

"Tempest, I'm worried about my mom. You have to get her out of the cells," Dazielle said. "I can't figure out why she confessed."

"Think about it. If you'd just heard the answers to my questions, wouldn't you think Hester could be covering for you?"

Her mouth dropped open, and her face paled. "Mom thinks I'm a killer?"

"You've got a great motive, and you had the opportunity to kill Irin. And no one I've spoken to so far can say where you were at the time of Irin's death. Your mom could have panicked and protected you."

Tears filled Dazielle's eyes. "I'm not sure she cares about me enough to stop me from going to prison."

"That's not true," Lailah said. "Your mom loves you. Moms just have different ways of expressing their fondness for their children."

"I guess." Dazielle bit her bottom lip as she stared at me. "Do you think that's why she did it?"

"That's the only reason I can think of her confessing to a crime she didn't do."

"My mom... she really loves me that much?"

"Of course she does," Lailah said.

"She never tells me." Dazielle's voice was just a whisper. "I never feel like I'm good enough for her."

"Oh, Dazielle. You are. And her sacrificing her freedom is proof," Lailah said.

Dazielle swallowed. "Tempest, you have to let her go."

"I will. Once we've found the real killer." It was unnerving to see Dazielle look so lost. "Is there anyone you can think of we should speak to as a priority? I've already got her boyfriend, Elyon, and business partner, Felice, on the radar."

"Maybe Gadreel?" Dazielle said. "He worked with Irin."

"They didn't have a good relationship?"

"He didn't talk about Irin much. It was all a bit awkward after she recruited Gadreel to help with the privatization plans. I wasn't happy about it, and we argued about his job, but he was insistent he remain involved. He said the opportunity was too good to miss."

"Gadreel's on the suspect list," I said. "I'll see what he was doing around the time of the murder."

"Probably getting drunk." Wiggles jumped off the couch. Phantom was riding on his back and chewing on his ear. He nudged Dazielle's knee with his nose. "We'll find out who killed your friend. Well, the person who wanted to ruin your career, destroy Angel Force, and make herself rich." He cocked his head. "Are you sure you didn't do it?"

"Completely sure!" Dazielle huffed out a breath, her expression softening. "You can take Phantom with you if you like. She already seems attached to you."

Wiggles tossed his head, and Phantom flipped off his back with an angry meow. "Nope. There's only room for one awesome animal in Tempest's life."

I smiled. "It's true. I have no vacancies for a magical ball of fluff. Dazielle, just keep your head down and don't do any investigating on your own. The higher angels won't like it since you've been suspended."

She shook her head. "I have to get my job back. I don't know what I'll do if I'm no longer working for Angel Force."

"We'll make sure you're back behind your desk in no time," Lailah said.

I stood and headed to the door. We said our goodbyes to Dazielle and headed out.

"What did you think of Dazielle's answers?" Lailah said.

"It's not looking good for her, but I'm not giving up. And Dazielle is a larger-than-life figure in law enforcement. You don't make friends doing her kind of work."

Lailah's eyes widened. "Someone killed Irin to make Dazielle look bad?"

"Why not? The killer picked a moment when Dazielle was alone and then struck."

"I never thought about criminals holding grudges. It makes sense, but the risk of upsetting them is worth it, to see wrongs righted."

"Absolutely. And that's what we focus on. We need to get a better picture of the remaining suspects and their connection to Dazielle."

"Where shall we go next?"

"The hotel. Let's find some guests to speak to."

Chapter 12

"You make the introductions," I said to Lailah as we walked to Tabitha's hotel. "I expect you know most of the wedding guests better than I do."

Lailah nodded. "I've met most of them once or twice at different events. Ceremony officiants get around."

I chuckled.

Her cheeks flushed. "I don't mean like that!"

"Of course not. You must meet interesting people doing your job."

"And not so interesting. There's always one person at an event who's the resident expert on something that's less than fascinating. I remember a painful conversation about the merits of different wax to make angel wings shine. I learned about fifteen different waxes! And I'm always too polite to tell anyone to put a sock in it."

There was a crash as we entered through the hotel door and then a low male laugh in a room off to our right.

Tabitha wasn't on the reception desk, so I headed along the corridor and poked my head around the door.

Lailah followed me. "That's Elyon. He was Irin's boyfriend."

I took a few seconds to admire the impressive physical form of the angel who was bent over picking up a bowl of fruit. He was muscular, blond, and wore a pair of faded dark jeans and an open-necked white shirt under a leather jacket. He was giving off some seriously rocker style angel vibes. I approved.

"He looks younger than Irin," I said.

Lailah nodded. "He is."

I put on my detective's hat, deciding it was unprofessional to leer too long at a suspect, and headed over to Elyon with Lailah and Wiggles.

He turned as we approached, his bright blue eyes looking bleary. "Sorry about the fruit. I'll pay for any damage. I knocked the bowl with my elbow. It was clumsy of me."

"Hi, Elyon. I don't know if you remember me. I'm Lailah. I officiated at the wedding yesterday."

Elyon squinted at her then nodded. "Sure. It was a great ceremony. I mean until Irin's murder. That wasn't so good." He reached for a glass of red wine and took a sip.

"I'm so sorry for your loss," Lailah said. "How are you coping?"

"With this." He raised his glass. "It's helping a lot."

"This is Tempest Crypt." Lailah gestured to me. "She's in charge of the investigation into Irin's murder."

Elyon's gaze ran over me. "The angels aren't investigating?"

"Not this time. It's a bit too close to home. I work freelance for them, and they asked me to give them a hand," I said.

"Sure. I guess that makes sense." He wiggled his fingers in my face. "Especially with that pretty mark on your forehead. I see you're in with the higher angels. Good for you."

"I know you were spoken to right after the murder, but I need to ask you a few more questions about Irin," I said. "Do you mind?"

"Of course not. I talked to an angel the night it happened. Then some scary witch told me not to leave the village or there'd be trouble. Does she work with you?"

I smiled. "In a way. My family was at the wedding, and they helped after Irin was discovered."

Elyon nodded. "Ask away. I've nothing better to do than drink and think, and that's always a bad combination."

"How long had you been together?"

"A couple of years."

"And what was your relationship like?"

Elyon shook his drink from side to side. "There's no point in lying about it. You'll only hear the truth from someone else. I wanted out of the relationship. I was done."

"Why did you want to end things with Irin?" I said.

"It was nothing bad. I mean, Irin was easy to be with, but I was tired of being a kept angel. It was fun at first, going to the posh parties and seeing how the other half lived. And she was generous most of the time. She'd buy me things and take me on vacations, but I realized we wanted different things."

"Irin wanted you to settle down with her?"

"No, she didn't want me to marry her." Elyon tossed back his hair. "She just wanted arm candy. It used to make my skin crawl how she'd parade me around parties and show me off to her friends. They'd paw at me like I was a toy to play with, not an angel with feelings. It was funny at first, and I played along and would flirt with them, but it got boring. Then the whole thing felt tired. I'm young. I want to go out, drink too much, dance with inappropriate supernaturals, and enjoy myself."

"And you couldn't do that at Irin's posh parties?"

"There was not a hope of any dance floor bump and grind or drunken foolishness. Irin wouldn't stand for it. She even limited the amount of alcohol I could drink. I got a three drink maximum, and that was only when I wasn't the chauffeur for her and all her braying friends."

"Did Irin know you were unhappy in the relationship?" I said.

"She didn't notice anything was wrong. Irin was focused on her career, so nothing else got her attention. Even when I turned down a couple of invitations to parties, she didn't ask me the reason. She simply hired someone good-looking to go with her."

"I hope you don't mind me asking, but were you only with Irin because she was wealthy?" Lailah said.

Elyon shrugged. "I was. She caught my eye because she was an attractive older angel, but the age difference became an issue. I think she got a thrill out of being with someone younger. And it was hot at first, being with an experienced angel to show me the ways of the world. I was into it. And I enjoyed her company. Irin was a clever angel, and she had big ideas about things."

"How did you feel when you learned about her murder?" I said.

"It was a shock, that's for sure. But then I realized I wouldn't miss her. It was a relief to know she was gone. She could no longer dress me up and parade me around like a piece of angel candy." Elyon sighed. "Although I'm wondering what to do now. Irin looked after me. She paid my bills and gave me a place to live rent free."

"You could find another sugar angel," I said.

He wrinkled his nose then glanced at Lailah. "You're pretty cute. Are you single?"

Lailah flushed bright pink and shook her head. "That's a bad idea. Ceremony officiants don't get paid anything like Irin. I wouldn't be able to keep you in the manner you're accustomed to."

"I'm done with those fancy parties and expensive gifts. Irin always said I should model, since I don't have the brain for anything else. Looking hot is my talent."

"She said that to your face?" I'd be tempted to kill someone if they were that rude to me.

"I didn't mind. I know where my assets lie, and it's not in the complicated business Irin did. And her work was her life. I guess that's why she wanted someone like me around. I didn't make demands on her time, I showed up when she needed me, and I entertained her friends."

"That wasn't enough for you?" I said.

"We both got something out of the relationship at first. But now she's gone, I feel like I've been released." Elyon took another sip of his drink. "I just need to figure out what I'm going to do with my life now Irin isn't propping me up. It's probably a good thing she's dead. It'll make me stand on my own two feet."

Lailah gasped and glanced at me.

Elyon sat upright. "No! I didn't mean that. I wouldn't wish anyone dead. It shouldn't have happened to Irin, and to have her wings taken was awful. It's an angel's worst nightmare to lose something so precious. I take that back. I'd rather Irin was alive, and I was stuck with her than that ever happened."

"Where were you when you learned about Irin's death?" I said.

Elyon looked around the room before his gaze settled on his glass. "Talking to one of Irin's business partners, Felice. Now, she's an angel you could have fun with. You must have noticed her at the ceremony. She was the only angel with auburn hair. She colors it because she likes to stand out. And it definitely gets my attention."

"You were just talking?"

"Yup."

"Are you certain about that, or were you looking for a new sugar angel while Irin was still alive?" I said.

He lifted his shoulders again. "I don't cheat, but I've got to take care of myself. I was thinking of calling time with Irin, and I needed a new path to follow. And Felice is so much fun. She's not as old as Irin and doesn't always talk about work. She also loves to party. So do I. I figured we could be compatible."

This angel wasn't as dumb as he made out, if he was planning to have another wealthy partner on the hook before he ditched Irin.

"Can you think of anyone who had a problem with Irin? Anyone who'd want to kill her in such a savage way?"

Elyon took a long sip of his drink. "I thought someone had been arrested for the murder?"

"We have someone we're holding, but we need to cover all the bases," I said.

"Irin had enemies, mainly because of her work. And she was ruffling feathers by suggesting changes to Angel Force. She talked to me about it, but I never paid much attention. Like I said, I don't have a business mind. I simply have a body made for pleasure." He winked at Lailah.

I resisted the urge to leer at that fine body. And Elyon had a point. You might as well use the assets the angels gave you.

"Thanks for your time," I said. "Don't make plans to leave Willow Tree Falls just yet."

"Err... okay. Do you think I'm a suspect?"

"You were close to the victim, and you admitted you weren't happy with your relationship. That's a motive."

"I was with Felice! Check my alibi." He looked at Lailah. "You believe me. You must!"

"There's nothing to worry about." Lailah patted his arm.

"We'll speak to Felice. Just don't go anywhere until we've done that," I said.

Elyon relaxed a fraction, although he still looked anxious. "I don't plan to. Not until I've figured out where I'll be staying once I leave here."

We said our goodbyes and headed back to the reception area to speak with Tabitha to see if Felice was in her room. She wasn't around, so we headed back out.

Lailah bounced along beside me, a big smile on her face. "I know I shouldn't be happy about being involved with this murder, but it's exciting. I've done nothing like this before. When I was in training, I thought about getting into law enforcement, but it never happened."

"It's always satisfying to find out who did it," I said. "And I hate it when justice isn't served or the wrong people get accused of crimes."

"Like Dazielle's mom?" Lailah said.

"Just like her."

"I'm happy you're letting me tag along. And I hope you don't mind me asking the occasional question. I get so excited by all the possibilities. It's so interesting pulling out people's motives and finding out where they were. Is it always this easy? Elyon was open about the problems he had with Irin."

"No, questioning suspects isn't usually that easy. People hide things, they fake alibis, and they don't always tell the truth, and sometimes they misdirect you. They think they heard something or saw something and it leads you down the wrong path."

"I'll help in any way I can to make sure we get to the truth."

"Thanks, Lailah. I'm glad to have you along. I usually just work with Wiggles, but as you've probably noticed, he gets distracted if there's any food around, or other animals, or if the wind blows in the wrong direction."

"I don't get distracted." Wiggles pulled his head from the trash can and hurried over to join us.

I plucked a piece of paper bag off his side and rolled it into a ball.

Lailah laughed. "What shall we do next? Find Felice?"

"Not today. I've got some family things to deal with, and I run a business, so I need to look in on that."

"Of course. How about we meet up tomorrow morning? We can continue then?"

"Good idea. Why don't you head back to Angel Force and check in on Hester? Maybe some time in a cell will have changed her mind about confessing to a murder she didn't do."

"Got it. Anything else?"

"Get the angels talking to as many guests as possible. We need to find someone who saw what Dazielle was doing at the time of the murder, so we can rule her out."

"I'll do that. See you back at Angel Force tomorrow at eight?"

I grinned at her and shook my head. "Let's make it nine-thirty. My club stays open late, and I need to put in an appearance tonight."

"It's a date. I'll bring breakfast." Lailah said goodbye, petted Wiggles on the head, and then walked away.

"I like her," Wiggles said.

"You would. She's always feeding you treats."

"Yeah, and she's being helpful to you. And she got you hot chocolate. You could consider having her as an assistant full-time, then I could relax more."

"You don't need any more time off to relax. Besides, Lailah has a job, and it's a handy one, given she knows everyone involved in this murder," I said. "Let's get to Cloven Hoof and check in with Merrie. I'll do a few hours of work, then we have to face off with my arguing sisters."

"Just don't forget my large order of steak," Wiggles said. "Lailah wouldn't forget to order my steak if she was coming along."

"You'll get your steak. Don't worry." And I'd find Irin's killer, once I'd dealt with my own problems.

Chapter 13

"I knew she'd be late." Aurora tapped her fingers on the table we sat at in Tilly's restaurant. "It's so typical of Zandra."

"She could have been held up by something," I said.

"Zandra's doing this to prove a point. She claims to be a rebel, but she's just a troublemaker. And she's causing trouble in the family."

"Let's not start the evening badly," I said. "Look at the menu. Food always makes you happy, so pick whatever you like."

Aurora grumbled under her breath as she studied the menu.

I looked out the window, trying hard not to frown. Zandra was twenty minutes late.

"Let's just order without her," Aurora said. "If Zandra decides to show up, she'll have to make do with whatever we order for her. I'm tempted to get her the green goddess garden salad with no dressing. Then maybe she'll realize she needs to show up on time if she wants to get a decent meal."

I watched as Wiggles trotted away from the restaurant door. Tilly never let him inside when there were other diners, so he'd be eating his steak outside.

His tail lifted, and I followed his gaze to see Zandra strolling along, not looking in any hurry to get here.

"She's here," I said to Aurora. "Try to be nice. I don't like you two arguing."

"Zandra's the one who always starts the arguments. You know me. I like everyone. But there's something about Zandra that rubs me the wrong way." Aurora tapped her fingers on my arm. "And have you noticed, she's always sparking with magic?"

"I have. And that's because, unlike us, Zandra didn't get a good magical education. She was pretty much left to fend for herself. So cut her some slack if her magic is unpredictable."

Aurora huffed out a breath. "That doesn't give her the right to be so mean to me. She came into my store the other day and said the cookies I left out for customers were dry. And she didn't even buy anything. Have you ever eaten one of my cookies and thought it was dry?"

"Your cookies are great. She was probably teasing you."

The restaurant door opened, and Zandra walked in. Tilly walked over to greet her and then led her to our table.

"You're late," Aurora said.

"I had things to do. I got here as soon as I could." Zandra sank into her seat. "What are we eating?"

Tilly stood beside the table, ready to take our order. "The special tonight is spinach and ricotta ravioli in a rich crab sauce. And there's also a partridge and parsnip pie with sweet potato mash."

"I don't want any of the fancy stuff," Zandra said. "I'll have a burger and fries."

Aurora tutted. She placed an order for the ravioli, while I ordered steak for Wiggles and a pie for myself.

Tilly headed off to the kitchen, and I concentrated on my sisters, who were glaring at each other.

Zandra glanced at me. "Have you figured out what you're going to do about Rhett?"

I shook my head. "Not yet."

"What's this about Rhett?" Aurora said. "I haven't seen him back in the village."

Zandra's smile was smug. "We saw him when we were out demon hunting together. He was skulking around looking all shady."

"You didn't tell me you'd seen him," Aurora said to me.

I narrowed my eyes at Zandra. Was she deliberately stirring? "I didn't mention it because it's not important. And I didn't speak to him. I just saw him on the street."

"I suggested we follow him, but no guy's worth chasing," Zandra said.

"You could have tried to speak to him," Aurora said. "What was he doing?"

"I already said," Zandra muttered. "He was skulking around."

"He wasn't skulking. But he looked like he had somewhere he needed to be," I said. "Besides, he knows where I am. If Rhett wants to speak to me, he can come for a visit."

Aurora's bottom lip jutted out. "You should have told me you'd seen him. I could have advised you what to do next."

"You'd have probably suggested Tempest propose to him," Zandra said.

"I don't know what you've got against marriage. I've never been happier since I became a married woman. Lex is a wonderful husband."

"Don't put me off my food," Zandra said. She looked at me. "You should ditch him, Tempest. Rhett's no good for you. No guy can be trusted."

"That's not true," Aurora said. "Rhett's always been loyal to Tempest, just like my Lex is with me." She grinned and examined the wedding ring on her finger.

"Being in a complicated relationship can make people do odd things," I said.

"Your relationship isn't complicated." Aurora tilted her head. "Or had Rhett been behaving oddly around you? Is this something else you haven't told me?"

Zandra chuckled and pretended to read through the wine list.

"Leaving the village without saying goodbye is odd," I said.

"He'll have a reason for that. I don't want you two to split up over something so small."

"I don't consider that small," Zandra said. "That's bad manners. The guy is a loser. Ditch him and find someone better. Or how about this? Try being single."

"Let's not keep talking about Rhett." I rearranged my cutlery and looked over at the kitchen, hopeful our food would arrive. "I've not been thinking about him. I've been too focused on Irin's murder."

"How are you getting on with the investigation?" Aurora said. "People are saying Dazielle's mom is in a cell. Is that true?"

I nodded. "She is. Hester confessed to killing Irin."

"But you don't believe her?"

"No. I think she's covering for someone."

Aurora's eyes widened. "Who?"

"Work it out, genius. You'd only confess to a murder you hadn't done to protect someone you loved," Zandra said. "There are a few options. Is Hester married?"

"Yes, but she doesn't like her husband much."

"So, she's not covering for her husband." Zandra thumped the table. "I've got it. It's Dazielle."

"That's a possibility," I said.

"That can't be right. Dazielle isn't a killer," Aurora said.

"Hester thinks otherwise."

Aurora shook her head. "Who else are you focused on? There have to be other suspects."

"Irin's boyfriend. I spoke to him today, and he wasn't all that sad about losing her."

"You think he did it?" Zandra said.

"Irin was his sugar angel. She was older than him and basically set him up. I got the impression he enjoyed it at first, but when he realized he was being used as a piece of meat, the shine faded."

"He wanted out of an unhappy relationship, and Irin wouldn't let him go?" Zandra said. "You think he offed her because of that?"

"It's a motive. And I've yet to check his alibi, so keep this quiet. Don't talk about this to anyone else until I've found the killer."

"Why go to the trouble of killing Irin, when he could have walked away like my dad did when things didn't work out with Mom?" Zandra said.

"That was different," Aurora said. "*Our* dad wasn't in his right mind when he left us and fooled around with your mom."

"They didn't fool around," Zandra growled.

"You weren't a proper family."

"Aurora! Be kind," I cautioned.

"Your lives weren't so perfect. He left you first," Zandra said.

Aurora glowered at her. "He was being magically influenced. Otherwise, he'd never have done that. Dad was happy with us."

"So you reckon," Zandra said. "I've been around your family long enough to know you're hard work."

"Our family is perfect! Take that back." Aurora smacked a hand on the table, and magic sparked across the white cloth.

"I speak as I find. Your granny Dottie is crazy, and your auntie Queenie—"

"Enough! Zandra, you're out of order."

"You tell her," Aurora said.

"You're just as bad!" I said. "Zandra, we've been nothing but kind since you came to the village. I know our family can be full on, but their intentions are good."

"They keep snooping on me and sending me food, acting like I don't know how to look after myself. And they keep asking if I want a hand with my spells." Zandra shrugged. "It's too much. They're way too intense."

"Maybe it feels weird they're always offering to help, but take them up on their offers. They're all powerful witches and want to make you a better witch."

"I'm fine as I am."

I shook my head. "You know that's not true. Your magic is getting noticed for all the wrong reasons."

"You'll end up in a cell just like Dazielle's mom if you're not careful," Aurora said. "Although maybe that's the best place for you."

Tilly arrived with our food, and I was glad of the distraction from the growing tension around the table. This sister kiss and make-up session was about as smooth as one of Granny Dottie's rum cocktails.

"I've got Wiggles' steak," Tilly said. "I'll take it out to him before he makes a hole in the door trying to get in. And I'd better hurry. The drool on the window is putting off the other guests."

"Thanks, Tilly. He'll love you for that."

No one spoke for several minutes as we ate our meals.

I set down my knife and fork. "Zandra, we're family. We look out for each other."

She shrugged again. "I don't need anyone looking out for me."

"You're not used to it, but try it. It's not so bad."

She ate a handful of fries and stared out the window.

Aurora arched her eyebrows at me.

I ignored her. We'd get through to Zandra, eventually.

No one spoke for several tense minutes. At least the food was good, so I could enjoy my meal.

"How about this for a theory for your murder?" Zandra looked over at me. "Just like our dad could have been influenced by magic, maybe the same thing happened to the victim's boyfriend. What if he was made to kill Irin?"

I mulled over the possibility as I ate the last of my pie. "It's an interesting idea. He seemed a little drunk when I spoke to him. I thought he was drowning his sorrows, but maybe his behavior was because of the aftereffects of a spell, and not the red wine."

"Can angel magic make others do their bidding?" Zandra said.

"Most likely, although none of them have ever tried it on me."

"That you know of," Zandra said.

"I don't like that idea," Aurora said.

"No surprise there. If I said puppies were cute, you'd disagree with me."

"Stop bickering," I said. "It's a theory to consider, but I think this murder was personal. All the angels get twitchy at the thought of having their wings taken. Whoever did this wanted to make a point. They took away Irin's wings."

"Because they didn't think Irin was a proper angel?" Aurora said.

"That could be the reason. And she was planning to interfere with Angel Force. It made a lot of angels unhappy." I finished my meal and pushed my plate away. I looked out the window to check on Wiggles. The steak was gone, and his gaze was fixed on the glass case of desserts.

"Is everyone done?" I said.

"Oh! No dessert?" Aurora pouted.

"I can't fit one in."

Zandra smirked. "There's always room for dessert."

"You like puddings?" Aurora's eyebrows rose. "I didn't think you would."

"Sure. Who doesn't? And I love anything with cream. Add in some chocolate and I'm always happy."

Aurora blinked rapidly. "I make a great chocolate cream torte."

"That doesn't sound terrible."

I glanced from sister to sister. Was a shared love of dessert a way to get them to bond? "Aurora's torte is amazing."

Zandra looked at the desserts in the glass case. "I'd be up for trying some when you have a piece going spare."

"I'll make you a whole one," Aurora said.

"There's no need to go to any trouble."

Aurora's smile was tentative. "I'd like to."

"You won't regret it," I said to Zandra. "Just leave some for me."

"I make no promises," Zandra said. "Let's order that strawberry pavlova. We can get the whole thing and share it."

"Oooh! Yes, Tilly does an amazing pavlova. Although her chocolate cinnamon brownie with ice cream is also great."

I sat back and grinned as they continued to discuss the desserts. It was so simple. Entice my sisters with treats, and they suddenly liked each other.

"We can eat that and work on more theories for your case," Zandra said.

Aurora nodded. "We'll draw up a short list of people close to Irin who might have wanted her dead."

"You should both get into law enforcement," I said. "You're good at coming up with ideas to help with this mystery."

"No, that career path isn't for me. I couldn't stand being around the angels all the time," Zandra said. "All those feathers make my nose itch."

"They're not so bad," Aurora said. "I used to date a half-angel."

"What happened to him?"

Aurora's cheeks flushed. "He was murdered."

Zandra snorted a laugh. "Did you do it?"

"Of course not!"

"Although Aurora was a prime suspect for a while," I said. "That's how I got into working with the angels. They wanted to charge Aurora with murder, and I was having none of it."

"Because you knew I was innocent," Aurora said. "As if anyone could think I'd ever murder someone." She looked at Zandra, and her eyes narrowed.

I chuckled. "The thought never entered my head. Let's order that dessert."

It looked like I still had some work to do before my sisters called a permanent truce, but at least we were making progress.

Chapter 14

I headed into Angel Force the next morning with Wiggles. It was a bright, sunny day, the club had been bouncing last night, and my mood was positive. Today was the day I'd figure out this murder.

"Hey, Dominic. What are you doing here?" I strolled over to his desk. He was back in his white uniform, a pile of paperwork in front of him.

He looked up and grinned. "I've been reinstated. I got the call last night."

"From Dazielle?"

Dominic shook his head. "No, it was another angel. Someone high up. They looked into the reason I was fired and decided it was unacceptable. From what I understand, they're looking at a lot of the work Dazielle's been doing over the last year. They said they had some concerns about her suitability as a leader."

"That's bad news. Does Dazielle know that's happening?"

"I'm not sure. I reached out to see if I could help her, but she wants nothing to do with me." He looked at the gold band on his finger. "It's a shame.

I'm married to her, and she won't even talk to me. I didn't think this would be how I'd start my married life."

I patted his shoulder. "Hang in there. Things will get sorted soon. I'm working on Irin's murder today."

He pressed his lips together then beckoned me closer. "I'm not supposed to ask you questions about the murder investigation. It was a condition of me coming back. And I'm not allowed to work on Irin's murder. The angels think I'm too close to it."

"That makes sense. Since she's confessed to the crime, your new mom-in-law is the prime suspect."

"Oh! Yes. I can't get used to thinking about her like that. Are you planning on charging Hester today?"

I arched an eyebrow. "Isn't that a question about the murder?"

Dominic grimaced. "Forget I asked. I don't want to lose this job again." He glanced around to make sure no one was listening.

"How about I tell you answers to things you might be interested in? Or at least, keep you in the loop so you don't feel left out?"

His smile was dazzling. "That's a great idea. You're so smart, Tempest."

"Not really. But I don't think Hester did it. I was hoping she'd change her mind overnight after a stay in the cells. It should have convinced her prison life isn't for her."

"As far as I know, Hester's still saying she did it. And I still can't figure out why."

"I've got a few ideas. I'll get this sorted out."

The main door into the open-plan office opened, and Lailah hurried in. She carried a tray of takeout coffees in one hand and balanced a huge box in the other.

I hurried over and grabbed the box, inhaling a delicious smell of sugar and sweet spices.

"Thanks." She shook out her hand. "I was getting a cramp. Those breakfast pastries are heavy."

"Did you hurt yourself?" I pointed at her wrist, which was wrapped in a bandage.

She looked at it and laughed. "That was my fault. I tend to pet animals first and ask if it's okay to do so later. I picked the wrong cat this morning while I was getting the food. That's why I'm late. She looked like such a sweet little thing, but then the claws came out, and she stuck them in my hand."

Wiggles trotted over. "You should follow my motto. Never trust a cat, especially not the ones around here. They tend to turn into something evil if you say the wrong thing to them. Or they're already evil and hiding in their cute, fluffy disguises."

"I can't help myself. I love all animals," Lailah said. "And you can't dislike all cats. You seemed to think Phantom was okay when you met her."

"She was an exception. I humored her because she's young. When she gets bigger, she won't get a free pass to chew my ears or ride around on my back like I'm her plaything."

"Let's get to work," I said. "We need to find out everything we can about Irin. I want to know the extent of her wealth, how much influence she had, and find out exactly what her plans were for Angel Force."

"Set me to work, boss," Lailah said. "I'll do whatever you need me to do."

By the end of the morning, I had a much clearer picture of Irin. I'd gathered a small team of angels in an interview room and stood in front of them, wondering where to begin. I'd recruited Cassiel, Jophiel, and Oriel to help on the case, alongside Lailah and Wiggles.

Lailah smiled at me from her seat and gave me a discreet thumbs-up.

"Thanks for the work you've done so far," I said.

Cassiel grumbled, while Jophiel smiled at me, and Oriel held a pen poised over a notebook, ready to write.

"Irin was an influential angel, with connections to many powerful individuals. And not only that, she had connections to other supernaturals. As a result, the higher angels want this investigation wrapped up quickly," I said.

"Irin had big plans to shake up Angel Force," Jophiel said.

"What did you all think about those plans?" I said.

"I like things how they are," Cassiel said. "Why change something if it works?"

"I heard we'd be getting pay rises," Oriel said, her voice soft and hard to hear. "And flexible working."

There were murmurs of agreement.

"I heard there'd be job losses," Cassiel said. "Fewer angels would be employed, so there'd be more money to go around. But I don't want to lose my job so someone gets a pay raise."

"There'll be additional training and more promotion opportunities," Jophiel said. "And I also like the idea of flexible working."

Cassiel crossed her arms over her chest. "I don't trust the plans. Irin could have been spinning lies to get the higher angels to agree to what she wanted."

Cassiel was old school, just like Dazielle, so I understood why she was hesitant to embrace this change.

"What didn't you trust?" I said.

"There were too many things leaving our control. Outsourcing protection, basic wish fulfilment, defeating lesser evils. Those are angel jobs."

"Tempest defeats demons for you all the time," Wiggles said. "You have no problem working with her."

"I wouldn't say that," Cassiel said. "And Tempest is an unusual example, given her own demon situation. She knows things that are useful to us, so I have no objection to exploiting her skills."

"I'm glad to be of service," I said dryly. "It sounds like Irin's plans divided the angels, and I suspect she made enemies as she developed her modernization ideas."

"And some of those enemies were at Dazielle and Dominic's wedding," Jophiel said.

"I have a question." Oriel raised a hand. "Why hasn't Hester been charged? We already have her confession."

"But that's all we have. No one saw Hester kill Irin. We have no murder weapon, and I'm not certain of her motive."

"Who do you think did it?" Jophiel said.

My gaze drifted from angel to angel. "I don't want anyone to attack me for saying this, but Dazielle had an opportunity, and she had a strong motive for wanting Irin dead."

The room erupted into protests, and even meek little Oriel looked unimpressed.

"That doesn't mean I want it to be right." I held up my hands and waited for silence. "Dazielle can be a massive jerk, but I also don't think she's a killer. The problem is, everything we've uncovered so far points to her as the murderer."

Lailah stood and joined me. "I have to agree with Tempest. And we still haven't found anyone who saw Dazielle around the time of the murder. Things don't look great for her, but none of us see her as a cold-blooded killer."

"And on her wedding day?" Cassiel gave a snort of disbelief. "She wouldn't have been able to do it. Someone would have seen the bride running away in a bloodied dress and carrying a huge knife."

"Dazielle was in the garden when Irin was found. She was on her own, and no one saw what she was doing," I said.

"That still doesn't mean she did it," Cassiel said. "I took several breaks from the loud music at the reception and went outside on my own. Does that mean I also go on the suspect list?"

"It might." I pursed my lips. "You don't think much of Irin's plans to change Angel Force."

Cassiel glowered at me and muttered something under her breath that sounded a lot like *idiot witch*.

"That's why we're still looking at other suspects," I said. "And now we have a better understanding of Irin's influence, it's easy to see how she'd have collected enemies over the years. She was ambitious and would have trodden on toes to get where she was."

There were nods of agreement.

I looked at Cassiel. "Only a supernatural with significant power would have been able to slice off Irin's wings, is that right?"

She nodded. "A powerful demon could do it. And I suppose a strong witch if she used the right weapon."

"An angel could do it as well," Oriel whispered.

"But your average knife couldn't be used to slice off wings?" I said.

Cassiel shook her head. "It wouldn't be possible. It would have to be something containing strong magic."

No one spoke for a moment.

Oriel cleared her throat. "An angel scythe would work."

"I've not heard of that weapon before," I said. "Tell me about it."

She glanced around the group. "It's a blade forged in demon fire. They're illegal to make these days, but demons still have a way of sneakily using them. It would easily slice through angel wings."

The angels shuddered and wrapped their wings around themselves.

"Are the cut marks on Irin's back consistent with using an angel scythe?" I said to Cassiel.

"It would fit. But I can't say conclusively that was the murder weapon."

"Where would you find such a weapon?"

"You can get them on the black market. If you speak to the right demon, they'll get you that sort of thing," Jophiel said.

"Is there anyone around here who could get their hands on an angel scythe?" I asked.

"Axel," Cassiel said. "His dad has connections in the demon world."

"Axel's been away for weeks. I know, because Merrie is pining for him. He's not involved in this." I tapped my foot on the floor. "We have a possible murder weapon, although we still need to find it."

"A team has checked the grounds, and there was no sign of any weapon," Jophiel said.

"We'll expand the search area to the whole village," I said. "I'll get a team out."

"What do you want us to do?" Lailah said.

"Jophiel, try to make contact with Felice. I need to speak to her about Elyon's alibi. And since she worked with Irin, she could have useful information for us."

"I'm on it. I'll head over there and see if Felice is about."

"Thanks. I also want to interview Gadreel. Oriel, get in touch with him and arrange for him to come in as soon as possible."

She nodded.

"Cassiel, will you re-check the wounds on Irin to see if you can confirm an angel scythe was used?"

"No."

I turned to her. "Because..."

"I can't make that determination. It's only a possibility that was the murder weapon, and angel scythes are rare. It would be a waste of my time."

"Take a look anyway, just in case something was missed."

That request earned me more grumbling insults.

"Good work, everyone. Let's... go solve a murder." I'd be glad when I wasn't in charge of the angels. It felt weird and unnatural to give them orders. I couldn't figure out how Dazielle thrived in this job.

The angels left the room, but I gestured for Lailah to stay with me. I closed the door once the last angel had gone and turned to her. "I have a job we need to do, and I don't want the others to know about it."

Lailah's pale blue eyes gleamed with excitement. "I love detective work. What do we need to do?"

"Search Dazielle's office."

Her smile faltered. "Do you think there's something in there to point to her being the killer?"

"I'm really hoping not, but we need to discount the possibility. Can I trust you to be discreet about this? It'll cause unrest in the team if they know I'm seriously looking at Dazielle as the killer, but I can't ignore all the signs pointing to her."

"My lips are sealed. Do you want me to help with the search, or should I cause a distraction so the other angels don't see what you're doing?"

"How about you act as a lookout? We'll go in there, and I can pretend to work while I have a poke around."

"I can cause a distraction," Wiggles said. "Most of the angels have brought in packed lunches today. I'll go on a food hunt. It drives them crazy when I borrow their food."

"Just don't cause too much chaos when you snaffle their lunches."

"Gentle chaos. Got it."

I headed out of the interview room and walked to Dazielle's office. I left Wiggles snuffling around and then shut the office door. Lailah stood in front of it, while I had a general look around, leafing through files and paperwork on the cabinets.

I checked through each cabinet drawer. Everything was neat and ordered, as I'd expect from Dazielle.

"Have you found anything useful?" Lailah said.

"Thankfully, nothing has shown up." I closed a cabinet drawer. "But I can't shake off the feeling I caught Hester doing something in here she shouldn't. It was just before she confessed to the murder. You took me to see the higher angels, and when we came back, she immediately confessed. I wondered if she'd found something that made her panic and think Dazielle could be the killer."

"Like what? Not the angel scythe?"

"That's just a possible murder weapon. And they sound rare, so we could be making assumptions. Would you know how to find an angel scythe?"

Lailah shook her head. "They were banned hundreds of years ago."

I searched through the desk drawers next. Dazielle had her pens arranged in color order and size. I went through the next drawer, which contained spare paper and envelopes.

I tugged open the bottom drawer. There was a file inside. On the front cover was a dried red smear.

I carefully lifted it out and set it on the desk. "Lailah, what does this look like to you?"

"Um... a stain of some kind?"

"Dazielle wouldn't leave this file with a stain on it. She'd replace the cover. Get this to Cassiel. I want to know what the residue is."

"Of course. What do you think it could be?"

"It looks like dried blood."

Lailah's face paled. "Oh! I'll do it right away. What are you going to do?"

"Visit a friend."

I headed out of Angel Force and hurried to Dazielle's apartment with Wiggles, my stomach churning.

"Do you really think that mark was blood?" Wiggles said.

"Maybe. I don't know. I'm hoping if we talk to Dazielle, just the two of us, she might open up more. She could have been holding back because we had Lailah with us. I could tell she was ashamed about the whole sham wedding situation when we visited."

"If we're going to her apartment, does that mean I have to play with that horrible kitten again?"

"You adored that horrible kitten. And Phantom is just what Dazielle needs. So long as we can keep her out of prison, they'll be great for each other."

We reached Dazielle's apartment, and I knocked on the door

It was opened to reveal a glum looking Dazielle. "Are you here to arrest me?"

"No. At least, not yet. But we need to talk."

"I figured you'd be back. Come in." Dazielle led us into the living room, and we all sat.

"Even though I didn't kill Irin, I feel guilty," Dazielle said.

"If it's any comfort, I'm not sure you did it. But I'm not going to lie, things don't look great for you. You have no alibi anyone can support, you had several public disagreements with Irin, and you stand to lose a lot if her plans went through."

"I know. You should lock me away now."

Wiggles snuffled around the living room, his butt waggling as he mooched about.

"Phantom's asleep if you're looking for her," Dazielle said. "She's in the bedroom."

He nodded but kept sniffing.

"I found something in your office that's made me worried," I said.

"What did you find?"

"Your bottom right-hand drawer has a file in it."

"Why are you poking about in my office?"

"It's a method I'm using to prove you're innocent. Why? Have you got something to hide?"

"No! And that file isn't important. I keep old clippings of cases that Angel Force closes. I bring them out during meetings. The angels like to hear positive news. People are so quick to point out when we do something wrong. I like to give them a boost and remind them what a great team they are."

"I'm not so interested in the contents of the file, but there was a stain on the front of it. Where did that come from?"

"A stain?" Dazielle shook her head. "There shouldn't be a stain on it. I keep my office tidy."

"There was. And I've asked Cassiel to analyze it."

"Why? What do you think it is?"

"That's what I want you to tell me. I was hoping you'd say you dropped a strawberry tart on it and didn't clean it off properly."

"Does that sound like me?"

I shook my head. "Do the other angels have access to your office?"

"Of course. I don't keep it locked. I trust them not to poke around. They're well-trained, so they wouldn't do that."

"They'd have no reason to go in that drawer and use the file? I wondered if someone else left that stain on it."

"There'd be no reason for them to touch that file." She leaned forward. "Tell me what you're concerned about."

"I don't want to jump to conclusions, but the stain looked like dried blood."

Dazielle blinked. "I'll be back in a minute. I don't feel so good." She hurried out of the room.

I looked around the living room while I waited for her to return. Wiggles had vanished from sight.

"Wiggles. What are you doing?"

"Smelling bad things. You need to get over here."

I stood and walked around to the back of the couch. Wiggles was sniffing a wooden box that sat to one side of it.

"Phantom's not in that box. She's in the bedroom."

"It's not a Phantom smell I've sniffed out. The second I came in here, I picked up on an odd scent."

"And it's in that box?" I glanced in the direction Dazielle had gone. "You should wait until Dazielle comes back. She won't like you poking around in her things. You know how uptight she is about anyone touching her stuff."

"You should look while she's not in here. It doesn't smell too good."

I eased open the lid of the box. There was a blanket on the top. I lifted it up, and my mouth dropped open. Beneath the blanket was a bloody scythe. It had a white handle with pearls embedded in it.

"Sorry for running out on you. I just... what are you doing?" Dazielle stopped by the couch.

I pointed at the scythe. "Dazielle, get over here and explain why the murder weapon is in this box."

Chapter 15

"What are you talking about?" Dazielle hurried over and stopped beside me. Her face turned several shades of green, before her hand flew to her mouth.

"That looks very much like an angel scythe," I said.

Dazielle gulped and staggered back. She dropped to her knees, and her wings drooped.

Wiggles trotted over, buried himself between the feathers, and licked Dazielle's face.

She didn't stop him, which showed how shocked she was.

I was about to kneel next to Dazielle, when there was a sad little meow from behind the bedroom door. I walked over and opened it.

Phantom bounced out, and her little white tail shot up in the air. She stopped when she saw Dazielle on the floor. She bounded over and leaped on her back.

I returned to Dazielle and sat in front of her. "Talk to me. How come the angel scythe is in your apartment and it's covered in dried blood?"

She lowered her wings and gently pushed Wiggles away. "I don't know. I've never seen that before."

"You're saying it doesn't belong to you?"

"Why would I have such a deadly weapon in my home? And angel scythes are illegal. You get in trouble if you possess one."

"Come take a closer look at it. Just don't touch it."

"I know not to touch evidence. I definitely don't want my fingerprints on that." Dazielle crawled over and peered into the box, her breath coming out in short bursts. "What should I do?"

"Try not to panic."

"It's too late for that."

"Why is it in this box?"

Her terrified gaze lifted to me. "I'm being set up. That must be it. This isn't mine. I've never seen it before."

"Who would want to set you up for this murder?"

She threw her hands in the air, making Phantom squeak. "I don't know! But someone has. I've arrested plenty of supernaturals over the years. One of them has come back to get their revenge."

"But who? Someone at your wedding?"

"No one from the wedding would do this to me."

"Are you certain? There were no angel guests who didn't like the way you run things around here?"

"I've fallen out with a few angels, but never over anything serious, and certainly nothing worth framing me for murder. No one hates me that much."

"Things weren't great between you and Irin. It shows you can have enemies."

"That was different. I was protecting Angel Force. I had to fight to preserve it."

"Some people might think you fought too hard, and things got out of hand."

"Yes, I suppose they might. What shall I do?" she whispered.

I rested a hand on her shoulder. I was worried about Dazielle. "What about anyone who could have snuck into the wedding? An unhappy supernatural who's recently been released from jail? Does anyone come to mind?"

"Not that I know of. And I'm always kept informed of inmate releases, especially if there's any likelihood they'll cause trouble." Dazielle looked up at me, and there were tears in her eyes. "You have to take me in. And you have to report this evidence."

"I will, but let's not be too hasty. You said the scythe was planted, so let's take a minute to figure out who planted it. Who has access to your apartment?"

"Just me."

"No one else has a set of keys?"

Dazielle shook her head. "No. I value my privacy. There's no one around here I'd trust enough to come into the apartment when I'm not here."

"You might need to rethink that now you have Phantom," I said. "Especially if you're planning any trips away."

"Or you could make her the office kitten mascot," Wiggles said. "She'd have fun with all the feathers floating around."

Phantom bounced up and down on Dazielle's shoulder as if she knew she was being talked about.

"Phantom's future will be out of my hands once I'm sent away for murder," Dazielle said.

"Phantom will be fine. And so will you. What about your neighbors? You don't leave a key with them so they can come and check on things when you're away?"

"There's no point. How often do I go away? I occasionally have to attend training sessions or meetings out of Willow Tree Falls but not frequently enough to have a neighbor drop by."

"Have you noticed any doors or windows open when they shouldn't be? Someone could have snuck in."

"I always lock my front door once I'm home. I sometimes have the windows open, but not wide enough for anyone to climb through. And I've been here most of the time. I'd have heard if anyone crept in."

"They could have used magic to make sure you didn't hear them. Someone could have crept in the window under a cloaking spell."

Dazielle's eyes narrowed. "Do you think a witch is trying to frame me?"

"I'm just making suggestions and trying to find a way out for you."

"The only witch around here who doesn't like me is you."

"Dazielle, be nice! I'm trying to help you. And we've both agreed we don't hate each other anymore."

She sighed. "I'm sorry. I'm so stressed, I can't think straight."

I closed the box lid. "Stay here. I'll look around and see if there are any signs of a break-in."

"You're wasting your time. I'd know if someone had been in here."

I hurried away and checked each window. They were all locked. If someone got in through one of these, they'd need to be good at climbing since we were up so high. I also looked for signs of a window being forced, but there was nothing to suggest anyone had gotten in that way. The front door was the same.

With a heavy heart, I returned to Dazielle. "I found nothing useful."

"I said you wouldn't."

I sat back on the floor in front of her. "Dazielle, I have to ask, and be honest with me, did you kill Irin? You had a moment of madness and lost control?"

She shook her head. "I didn't, but it looks like I did. And you've already told me how terrible my alibi is and that I have a great motive. It's only logical I did it. Irin was becoming a problem for me, so I got rid of her."

I sighed. I was out of options. "I'm really sorry to have to do this, but I've got to take you in to Angel Force."

Dazielle swallowed and nodded. "So that's it? You're giving up the search for anyone else?"

"Not yet. There are still a few stones I've yet to turn over and see what slithers out. But with the murder weapon in your apartment, what else should I do?"

"You could let me run away?" Her gaze flashed to the window. "I could start a new life somewhere no one knows me."

"And how long would that last? Knowing the higher angels, they'd send me after you. We wouldn't want our amazing friendship to end in a fiery showdown."

"I'd like to see you try to take me down."

I smiled at her. "I'll take you in, get the angels over here to collect the angel scythe, and then we'll go from there. I'm still not charging you with anything."

Dazielle stood, her legs looking shaky. Phantom was perched on her shoulder, and she licked her face.

Dazielle scooped her up, gave her a kiss on the head, and then handed her to me. "Can you look after Phantom?"

"Sure. I'll check in on her and feed her if you like."

"No, she's used to me being around. You need to take her back to your apartment so she has company."

"Are you sure she'll come with me?"

"I'll look after her," Wiggles said.

Tears trickled down Dazielle's cheeks. "I'm always so horrible to you, Wiggles, but you're really not that bad for a hellhound."

He wagged his tail. "And you're not so terrible for an angel."

I passed him Phantom, and she happily bounced onto Wiggles' back.

"Let's go," I said to Dazielle.

We headed out of the apartment and over to Angel Force. I was pretty sure Dazielle wouldn't make good on her suggestion to run, but I kept a close eye on her, anyway.

We headed through the doors, and all the angels turned to look as we entered the main office.

Dazielle hung her head and wouldn't meet anyone's gaze.

I sucked in a breath, not looking forward to issuing my next order. "Jophiel, I need you to put Dazielle in a cell."

Her eyes widened. "Of course. But why?"

Cassiel appeared, looking grumpy. "What's going on?"

"Cassiel, I need you to go to Dazielle's apartment. We've discovered a weapon there. You need to examine it."

"A weapon?" Cassiel crossed her arms over her chest. "You're bringing Dazielle in because you think she killed Irin?"

"Don't argue with Tempest," Dazielle said. "Just collect the evidence. It's in the blanket box by the side of the couch."

Cassiel's mouth opened, then she snapped it shut. "Whatever you say, boss." She took Dazielle's keys and went off to collect an evidence kit.

"What about my mom?" Dazielle said. "If I did it, then you can let her go."

"I need to speak to her before I do that."

Jophiel led Dazielle away, her head down as she did the walk of shame to the cells.

Lailah raced over, her cheeks flushed. "I just heard. Have you really brought Dazielle in for Irin's murder?"

I nodded. "I went over to have a chat with her, and Wiggles sniffed out what's most likely the murder weapon. It was an angel scythe, and it's covered in blood."

Lailah looked over at the cells. "I'm so shocked. Dazielle really did it?"

"Every piece of evidence points right at her. But I still don't understand how the angel at the center of attention on the night of the murder got away with it. Someone must have seen her slip off to kill Irin, or seen her with the weapon, or with blood on her hands." I rubbed my forehead.

"Come take a seat. I'll make some tea. It must have been a shock to discover the murder weapon."

I walked along behind Lailah, and she found a quiet corner of the office for us to sit in. "It was."

Lailah pushed me gently into a seat and then took a step back. "Is something on your mind?"

"It seems too easy. Why didn't Dazielle get rid of the scythe? She must have considered the possibility her apartment would get searched. The angel scythe was too easy to find."

Lailah made two mugs of tea and handed me one before sitting in a seat opposite me. "I don't know how you do it."

"Do what?"

"This crime solving is so intense. You must have trouble sleeping. I can't stop thinking through all the possibilities of what might have happened and who had the most to gain from killing Irin. It's been keeping me up."

"It has its moments, but it's not usually like this. And I'm not usually dealing with people I actually know. That adds a different layer of complicated."

Lailah sipped her tea. "I didn't want to say anything, but the higher angels have had concerns about Dazielle for some time."

"What kind of concerns?"

"They don't think she's handling responsibility well."

"Dazielle can be a giant idiot, but she's good at her job. She gets things round the wrong way, but she usually figures things out."

"What if her arranged marriage to Gadreel pushed her over the edge?"

I grimaced. "That's why I'm not keen on getting married. It's so stressful. My sister getting married was bad enough."

Lailah smiled. "You don't have a special someone you'd like to marry?"

I briefly thought about Rhett. "There's no one. How about you?"

"Not yet. But I'm always hopeful. It seems I'm always the officiant and never the bride."

"Elyon seemed interested in you. You weren't tempted?"

She giggled. "No! I don't think I'd be able to trust someone like that. I'd always be worried someone prettier would snatch him away."

"You're a catch. You'll find the right guy."

Lailah raised her mug to me. "I will. But I'm in no rush. And if marriage makes you snap like it did Dazielle, I'm tempted never to risk it."

"I don't know if it did."

We sat in silence and drank our tea. What was I missing? Who'd framed Dazielle? Or was I simply avoiding admitting that she was the killer because of our association?

Lailah touched my knee, bringing me out of my pondering. "We both know Hester is a demanding mom. Maybe Dazielle did break under the pressure."

I recalled how intense she'd been when I'd returned to the village. Could this wedding have sent her over the edge?

I shook my head. "And she killed Irin because of it? Why not go crazy at the ceremony? Punch Gadreel or set fire to something? Murder is extreme."

"Irin had everything Dazielle wanted. She was wealthy, had a gorgeous boyfriend, and had the ear of the higher angels. Dazielle could have been jealous. And her mom was putting so much pressure on her. Maybe it all got too much."

"If I didn't know Dazielle so well, I'd agree with you. Dazielle's work is her life, and she hated Irin's modernization plans. But as for being jealous of Irin having Elyon, I don't know about that. I'm not sure he's her type. I'm not even sure Dazielle has a type. She doesn't date."

"She didn't date when we were in college."

"Why was that?"

"Because she was attached to Gadreel," Lailah said. "Their union had been planned for a long time."

"Oh! Of course. I didn't think about that. If she was engaged to Gadreel, she wouldn't consider herself free to see other angels. Wow! That's terrible. She couldn't even have any fun because she was tied to an angel she loathed."

Lailah smiled. "Do you see what I mean? Dazielle's life is complicated and high stress. And stress messes with people. I don't want to say it was Dazielle who killed Irin, but..."

"But the evidence suggests otherwise. As does her motive and her opportunity." I downed the rest of my tea. "Help me figure this out, Lailah. If it was Dazielle, where did she get the scythe? You said those things are rare."

"Very rare. But if you know the right people, well, I suppose the wrong people, they'd know how to get their hands on a thing like that. And I imagine Dazielle comes across many crooked types in her work."

"I guess she does." Had she used her contacts to plan this out? Get the weapon, make sure Irin was alone, and then kill her?

"Another tea?" Lailah stood and took my empty mug.

I nodded. I didn't like to admit it, but things looked dire for Dazielle.

Chapter 16

"When are you going to charge me? You can't keep me in a cell and do nothing. It makes you look incompetent." Hester sat in front of me in the interview room. Her eyes were narrowed and her arms crossed over her chest. She looked like she'd aged about five years since I'd last seen her.

"I was making sure we had the right person for the murder." I sat opposite Hester. Lailah was next to me, and Wiggles was asleep in the corner, with Phantom draped over him.

"You're looking at the killer. Charge me and let's get this over with."

"Not just yet." I sucked in a breath. "We've found the murder weapon."

Hester's tongue darted across her lips. "I thought I'd hidden that, so you'd never find it."

"What did you do with it after you killed Irin?"

She blinked. "I... I don't remember. I was panicking and in shock. I definitely disposed of it."

"Did you throw it away in the garden? Did you drop it in the river? Maybe it was in your hotel room? Give us a clue."

"Like I said, my memory is bad. I've blanked some of that night out. Killing is traumatic. You can't expect me to remember every tiny detail."

"The murder weapon is a huge detail. Think hard. You cut off Irin's wings, then what? Did you run? Did you hear someone coming? Did you take anything from the scene?"

Hester gulped. "I... yes, I ran. Someone was coming toward me, and I didn't want to be found with the body."

"And the weapon you used? Was it in your hand or on the ground?"

"I... I don't recall."

I leaned forward. "You know exactly what happened that night. And you know it would have been impossible for you to kill Irin."

"It's very possible. I did it!"

"We've spoken to a number of wedding guests again. One of the questions we specifically asked was if any of them saw you. What do you think they told us?"

Hester fidgeted in her seat. "There was a lot of alcohol at the wedding. Those conversations won't be reliable, so you can't trust what you heard about me."

"I disagree. And several guests saw you just before Irin was killed. You were talking to a group of angels about the cost of the flowers. You came into the garden from the wedding reception, and that was the first time you saw the body."

Hester laid her hands flat on the table. "I could have killed Irin before that and returned to the wedding reception to cover my tracks."

"But you didn't. I have witnesses who confirm you were in the wedding reception for at least half an hour before Irin was murdered. And she'd only been dead a few minutes before her body was discovered."

"They made a mistake. And your timings are wrong. Re-examine your evidence, and you'll see I was very capable of doing it."

"Yet you can't remember what you did with the murder weapon?"

She paused. "No."

"And you have no recollection that you planted the murder weapon in your daughter's apartment?"

Hester's breath sounded like it got stuck in her throat as she gaped at me. "I did no such thing."

"Why did I find it in the apartment, if you didn't put it there?"

She jerked forward in her seat. "That can't be true. You're only saying that to confuse me. Dazielle has mentioned several times that you can be a difficult witch."

"Here's what I believe. You didn't kill Irin, but you think Dazielle did."

Hester shook her head but didn't say anything.

"What did you find in Dazielle's office that convinced you she was the killer?"

"Nothing!" Hester's panicked gaze flashed around the room. "I don't know what you're talking about."

"You were poking around when I walked in on you. And you were looking in her drawers. You also had a grip on your purse like you had your life savings in there and needed to protect it."

Hester looked down at the floor. "Have you really found the murder weapon?"

"Yes. It was an angel scythe."

A small moan slid from Hester's lips. "That's a terrible weapon to use. And it was in Dazielle's apartment?"

"Yes. We're running tests on it, but no one will be surprised when they find Irin's blood on the blade."

Hester was quiet for a long time, and I glanced at Lailah. I didn't want to push Hester any more than I had to, but it was obvious she was lying to protect Dazielle.

She cleared her throat. "I... I found an angel wing feather."

"A feather?"

"Yes, and it had blood on it. I panicked when I saw it in Dazielle's drawer. It was just lying on top of a folder for anyone to see. I had no idea what Dazielle was doing with a bloody angel feather in her possession, but I was so scared she was involved in killing Irin. Everyone knew they didn't like each other. I grabbed the feather and stuffed it in my purse. You walked in just after I'd done that."

"You took evidence that could have helped solve this murder," I said.

"I shouldn't have done that. But I had to protect my family."

"Did you already have your suspicions about Dazielle?"

"No, I didn't. And I was genuinely waiting for her that morning. I was simply looking around while I waited."

"You were snooping into her private business?"

Hester lifted her chin. "It's a mother's right to make sure her daughter isn't hiding things she shouldn't. And given how odd she's been over marrying Gadreel, or rather, marrying that adorable dumb blond sitting out in the office, I wasn't sure she was herself. I needed to make sure she had no more secrets that could cause the family problems."

I was tempted to reveal the true nature of Dazielle and Dominic's marriage, but that was an awkward conversation mother and daughter needed to have when a murder charge wasn't hanging over their heads.

"I know Dazielle thinks I push her too hard, but I've always wanted the best for her. I didn't think law enforcement was the best she could do," Hester said.

"Dazielle loves her work. I've never seen her happier than when she solves a crime. Why would you stop her from doing something that gives her so much satisfaction?"

Hester's mouth twisted to the side. "We have a reputation to maintain. Our family moves in certain social circles, and there have been disagreements among the angels over the last two decades. I wanted Dazielle to join me in strengthening our position and calming the situation. It was all laid out."

"But Dazielle had other plans?"

"I thought she'd get over her obsession with Angel Force and see what she could do by Gadreel's side. I also didn't expect her to want to marry for love." Hester flicked a hand in the air.

"Isn't that Dazielle's choice? Don't you want your daughter to be free to figure out what she wants out of life, even if it means dealing with criminals and hitching up with some adorable dumb blond? And by the way, Dominic is a sweetie. Dazielle could do a lot worse."

"Dazielle has an enviable position in Angel Force. We all respect her," Lailah said. "I'd be happy doing this kind of work."

Hester sighed. "She could have been so much more."

"And been miserable while she did it," I said. "Did Dazielle ever talk to you about how stressed she was about marrying Gadreel?"

"We had plenty of conversations about the marriage. She knew it was the right thing to do."

"The right thing for you or the right thing for her?"

Hester shrank back in her seat. "Dazielle never said she didn't want to marry him."

"Is that because you're as intimidating as an angry demon with a hangover, and she didn't want to let you down?"

Hester raised her thumb to her mouth and was about to chew on a nail. She dropped her hand back into her lap. "It's taken me years to stop biting my nails. I always do it when I'm stressed."

"Dazielle was stressed about her marriage to Gadreel. She didn't think it would make her happy," I said.

"She… she never told me that." Hester's eyes widened. "You don't think my actions made Dazielle do this, do you?"

I glanced at Lailah, and she raised her eyebrows. "We still don't know for certain Dazielle killed Irin, but I am certain you didn't do it. You lied about your alibi, and you concealed evidence that could have helped us."

Hester started chewing on a nail. "How much trouble am I in?"

"I'll have to consider that with the angels. Right now, you're free to go."

"You're releasing me? What about Dazielle?"

"She's already here. We're holding her in a cell while we look at the murder weapon and talk to the remaining suspects."

"Oh! There are other suspects? You still think there's a chance Dazielle didn't do this?"

I nodded. "She wasn't the only one who had a problem with Irin."

Hester grabbed my hand. "I'm begging you to help my daughter. You have influence and power. That mark on your forehead shows the strength you carry. And I'm aware of the demon that lives inside you. Only a powerful witch could contain such potent energies and not be ripped apart. Use your power to clear Dazielle's name. I'll do whatever you ask of me, but don't let Dazielle suffer."

I eased my hand out of her tight grip. "I'm not as powerful as you think."

Hester shook her head. "You are. And you need to use that power to make sure Dazielle isn't charged for this crime. She's innocent."

"Didn't you think she killed Irin, though?" Lailah said softly. "After all, you hid evidence and claimed you were the killer to keep her safe."

"Do you have children, Lailah?" Hester said sharply.

She shook her head. "Not yet."

"When you do, you'll learn there's a place in your heart you didn't even know existed. It's reserved for your children. The love you feel for them is the deepest and most enduring you'll ever experience, and you'll do anything to keep them free from harm. I know I'm not the most loving of mothers, not in the way some mothers are, but I always want the best for Dazielle. She deserves it, and that's why I push her so hard. When I discovered that bloody feather, my instincts kicked in. I didn't know why it was there, but I knew it shouldn't be. I took it to protect Dazielle, and I'd do it again. Even if I go to jail because of my actions, I don't regret it."

Lailah nodded. "I can tell you care very much for Dazielle."

"I do." Hester looked at me, a tear tracking down one cheek. "Which is why you must help her, Tempest. I've done what I can. Now it's up to you. My daughter's freedom is in your hands."

"I'll do what I can to help her." I looked at Lailah. "Show Hester out. And make sure she has all her things."

"I'd like to see Dazielle before I go," Hester said.

"She's not having visitors just yet," I said. "I'll let you know when you can visit."

Hester looked like she was about to protest then simply nodded and stood.

Wiggles yawned and rolled onto his back as they left the room, knocking Phantom off and making her hiss. "Would you do that for me?"

I looked down at him. "Hide evidence that showed you killed someone?"

"Yep. I think Hester's an awesome mom for covering for Dazielle."

"I'd cover for you." I leaned back in my seat. "It would take ages to train up another hellhound."

He huffed out smoke, and Phantom chased after it. "I'd have a great reason for bumping someone off. I would never mindlessly kill."

"I bet your motive would involve food."

"Most likely." His eyes glowed red. "You don't want to mess with me when there's only one cookie left in the jar."

I scooped up Phantom and petted her.

Wiggles trotted over and leaned against my leg. "What are we going to do about Dazielle?"

"She hasn't confessed to anything, despite the evidence suggesting she should. I'm clinging to that. And the few suspects we have left."

"We should get something to eat," Wiggles said. "I think better on a full stomach. And I'm stumped as to who the killer is. Something sweet will get my neurons firing."

"Good plan. Let's grab food, and then we take another look at Elyon, Felice, and Gadreel. I'm not done with them yet. Maybe I missed something that puts them in the garden, killing Irin."

"And puts Dazielle in the clear."

"We can always hope."

Chapter 17

The rest of the day was taken up by re-questioning wedding guests to see if anyone had seen Dazielle around the time of the murder or anything else suspicious that would point us to the remaining suspects.

No one could confirm Dazielle had been in the wedding reception at the right time, and the guests who'd been in the gardens couldn't confirm they'd seen her.

Our blushing, potentially murderous bride had done an excellent job of hiding at her own wedding at exactly the wrong time. I just needed one person who'd seen her, so I could discount Dazielle as a suspect.

I sat on a bench outside Mystic Mushroom with Wiggles and Lailah. We had two large takeout pizzas, which we were sharing between us.

"I still can't figure out how Dazielle had time to hide the angel scythe," I said.

Lailah nodded. "And why was that feather in her desk? Did she keep it as a souvenir?"

"If she was some kind of creepy serial killer, then that's a possibility, but this is Dazielle we're talking about. The angel is so neat, precise, and tidy. She'd freak out at the thought of a bloody trophy left in her desk, especially since it messed with her neat folder. If she had kept a trophy from her kill, she'd sterilize it and frame it behind glass so it fit her office aesthetic."

"If it wasn't Dazielle who put it there... then maybe her mom? Is this some kind of double bluff from Hester?"

"No, Hester is in the clear. I mean, she's not. She lied and stalled this whole investigation by claiming to be the killer, but Hester didn't murder Irin." I took a bite of pizza. "Someone planted that feather."

"And the scythe?"

"That too."

"Unless.... Dazielle really did it," Lailah said softly.

I sighed. "Yeah, that's always a horrible possibility. No! I can't believe it was Dazielle."

"Which means, we're looking for someone who has a big grudge against Dazielle. They somehow planted that feather in the hope it would be enough to shine the spotlight on her problems with Irin."

"But it wasn't enough, because Hester messed things up by taking away the planted evidence. So the real killer had to plant something else that left us in no doubt that Dazielle killed Irin."

"And what's more damning than finding the murder weapon?"

"Maybe the killer had no choice. Irin's body had been taken away, so they couldn't get more feathers to plant on Dazielle." I was warming up to the idea of Dazielle being framed. "They just needed to figure out a way into her apartment, so they could hide it."

"And without Dazielle knowing." Lailah shook her head. "How did they get in?"

I frowned. "There wasn't a way in. I checked when I went to see Dazielle. The place was locked up tight. There were no signs of a break-in, and Dazielle doesn't give keys out to anyone."

Lailah hummed under her breath. "There has to be a solution somewhere."

"Why wasn't the angel scythe destroyed?" I said. "Why did the killer keep it? They must have known the risk if they were found with it."

"I imagine it's not an easy thing to destroy," Lailah said. "Anything forged in demon fire is tough."

"The killer should have thrown it away somewhere hard to find."

"Maybe they didn't have a chance. They were disturbed just after they killed Irin, so they had to run off with the murder weapon."

"But no one was seen running away from the wedding reception. And no one was missing during the reception, other than Dazielle." I chewed on a bite of pizza, the delicious gooey cheese and fiery pepper not making me feel better.

"Look! There's Felice and Elyon."

I peered in the direction Lailah pointed. Elyon had an arm around Felice's waist and was whispering something in her ear that made her smile and kiss his cheek. "Those two seem cozy. Elyon didn't take long to move on."

"He said he was looking for a new sugar angel. But it seems fast. And disrespectful to Irin. She hasn't even had a funeral."

I finished my last bite of pizza and stood. "Let's talk to those two. I need to check Elyon's alibi, and we can find out exactly what Felice thought of her business partner."

We dashed after Elyon and Felice.

"Elyon, I'd like a word with you," I said.

He turned, and his eyes widened as he swiftly stepped away from Felice. "Of course. Have you got news about Irin?"

"I'm still investigating what happened to her. Why don't you introduce me to your friend?" I raised my eyebrows at the tall, curvy angel with glossy auburn hair and a silky blouse unbuttoned to way beyond decent.

"Oh! This is Felice. I was just... comforting her."

Felice fluttered huge dark lashes and flashed me a megawatt smile. "We were comforting each other. I also knew Irin."

"I'm glad I caught you both," I said. "We're almost ready to close this case and have eliminated almost all the suspects in the investigation."

"I'm confused," Elyon said. "There are multiple suspects?"

Felice giggled. "You get confused so easily, honey."

"I mean, I heard Hester was released, but Dazielle got arrested. Didn't one of them kill Irin? That's what everyone is saying."

"Dazielle's voluntarily come in for questioning. No one's been charged yet," I said.

Elyon glanced at Lailah. "So you still think the killer is out there?"

Lailah nodded.

"I'm not sure how I can help. You already know my story," Elyon said. "I was talking to Felice when we heard about the murder."

Felice nodded. "We were together. I can confirm that."

"Tell me about your relationship with Irin," I said to Felice.

"We were great pals and tight friends for years, but Irin changed recently. She became much more money focused. Angels shouldn't be into material things to bring them happiness." She smoothed a manicured hand down her designer blouse.

My gaze ran over her. "For someone who doesn't think material things bring happiness, you wear expensive clothing."

She giggled. "These are gifts from admirers. Men love to see me in high heels. They show off the curve of my leg. Don't you agree?" She turned a toned leg to one side and jutted out a hip.

"You look great. Was your friendship with Irin in trouble?"

"No, nothing like that. We just drifted apart. Our relationship became more of a professional one. I work in the public relations department of her business. I put the shine on everything. Give it some angel sparkle."

"Were you happy working with Irin?"

Felice glanced at Elyon. "I wasn't unhappy. I mean, I didn't always agree with how she ran things. But she was in charge, so I kept my head down and made sure everything looked amazing."

"What were you unhappy about?"

She pursed her glossy lips. "Irin sometimes cut corners. She became so driven to make as much money as possible that she ordered cheap things and then made the staff jazz them up so they looked expensive. I kept telling her you can't fake quality, but she never listened to me."

"That must have been frustrating."

"It was. I was thinking working for Irin wasn't such a good idea."

"Were you considering resigning?"

Felice smiled wickedly at Elyon. "I was thinking about taking a new path. Maybe even taking time off and having some fun with a special someone."

Elyon grinned but then attempted to look chastened when Lailah tutted her disapproval.

"What were you and Elyon doing together at the time of the murder?" I said.

"Oh, just talking. I'm a people person, so I was doing the rounds and chatting to everyone."

"You know Elyon well?"

"We've met many times. He usually attended events with Irin. We got to know each other well over the last year or so." Felice smoothed a hand down her hair.

"And what were you talking about?" I said.

"Wedding gossip. Nothing important." Felice glanced at Lailah and bit her lip.

Lailah touched my arm. "I... I think I could be useful here. I didn't say anything when we questioned Elyon at the hotel, but I saw him with Felice at the wedding reception."

I frowned at her. "Why keep that a secret?"

"Well, they weren't just talking." Lailah's cheeks glowed. "It would have been impossible for them to talk because of all the kissing they were doing. I walked in on them. They'd found a quiet room and were enjoying each other's company."

"This information would have been helpful a few days ago," I muttered.

"I know, and I am sorry." Lailah clasped her hands together. "I didn't want to say anything because they'd sworn me to secrecy."

Elyon and Felice looked at each other. Felice was also blushing.

"I didn't want Felice to get a bad reputation for stealing Elyon from under Irin's nose," Lailah said.

Felice's mouth twisted to the side. "Okay, we were doing more than chatting about the wedding, but that's not a crime. Elyon had told me several times he was done with Irin, and I was done talking about a relationship and wanted to take things to the next level. Who can resist this gorgeous face?" She ruffled Elyon's hair.

He wedged his hands into his pockets. "That's what happened. Lailah caught us, and I begged her not to say anything. I didn't want people thinking badly of Felice. And at the time, I was still with Irin. I'd come to the wedding with her. It would have looked bad if I'd snuck off with another angel. Neither of us meant any harm by being together."

"I doubt Irin would have agreed if she'd caught you," I said.

"Most likely not. But I was honest with you when we first spoke. I didn't want to be with Irin anymore and was moving on."

"So you didn't kill Irin; you just cheated on her," I said.

He sighed and glanced at Felice. "It's not my proudest moment, but Felice is too delicious."

"You're so adorable," Felice said. Her smile faded as she took in my expression. "Neither of us wanted Irin dead. I wasn't happy working with her, but there are plenty of opportunities out there for a qualified angel like me. I was looking around and weighing my options, just like Elyon. Neither of us were in a rush to move on completely until we'd found the perfect fit. As Irin always said, 'Don't take it personally; it's just business.'"

I was deeply unimpressed by all the secrecy going on, and I was disappointed in Lailah for keeping this information from me.

"Is there anything else we can do for you?" Felice said. "We were about to have dinner."

"That's all for now," I said.

"I hope you catch the killer soon. " Felice caught hold of Elyon's arm, and they walked away together.

I turned toward Lailah. "I can't work with you if you don't tell me everything you know. We could have discounted Felice and Elyon straightaway if you'd told me you'd seen them together."

She dropped her gaze. "I really am sorry about that. I didn't want to hide the information, but I hate breaking promises. Elyon was so panicked that word would get out about his affair with Felice, and I felt sorry for him. And after we interviewed him and he told you he was with Felice, I didn't see any harm in keeping the information about them kissing to myself."

"Is there any more information you know about suspects you need to share with me?"

"No, that's it. I won't do it again. I wish I'd told you the truth, but then I'd have felt terrible about breaking my word. I don't think there's anything bad about Elyon or Felice. They're just lust struck."

I sighed and watched Elyon and Felice as they headed into a restaurant. "It seems there are some angels around here who don't mind breaking their word. Elyon was more than happy to find himself a new honey, while keeping Irin on the hook."

"At least we've eliminated both of them."

"Unless they're covering for each other," I said. "Or they're both in on it."

"That's not possible. I was with them when word reached us about someone dying in the garden. And when I found them, they were very... involved with each other. I think they'd been in that room for a while."

"Okay, so we rule them out."

"Can I still work with you?" Lailah said. "I won't mess up again."

"Sure, but no more secrets." I pulled my hair off my face. After a day of interviewing, I'd gotten exactly nowhere. I needed some time out to clear my head and figure out what to do next.

"What shall we do now?"

"Let's call it a night. I've got some work to do at Cloven Hoof. We'll meet tomorrow morning at Angel Force."

"We still have Gadreel to speak to," Lailah said. "He could be our missing link."

"Let's hope he is," I said.

"See you tomorrow. I'll bring donuts."

I turned and walked away with Wiggles. I stomped along, my head full of theories about what happened to Irin. I couldn't get my thoughts around Dazielle being the killer, but I was almost out of options.

"Don't be angry with Lailah," Wiggles said. "She was being a typical angel and trying to do the right thing by everyone."

"I'm not angry with her, mainly disappointed. I should stick with you. At least I know what I'm getting."

"A sharp mind, a nose that sniffs out all the clues, and a killer instinct?"

"More like an obsession with food, terrible flatulence, and a nose that gets distracted by any morsel on the floor."

"Hey! I found the angel scythe. If my nose hadn't sniffed that out, we wouldn't have Dazielle in a cell about to be charged with murder."

"Which I'm not sure is such a great thing," I said. "I'm missing something in this case. I just need to find out what it is."

Chapter 18

I flipped the pancake, almost getting the whole thing back in the pan on the first attempt. I shook it around then set it back on the stove before turning to Wiggles. "Are you done with your breakfast already?"

"That kibble didn't even touch the sides. Besides, that was only the starter. You're making me pancakes, too, right?" Wiggles ducked as a white ball of sparking fur flew at him.

Phantom skidded across the kitchen floor and bashed into my legs. She looked up at me, meowed, then scaled my leg, digging her tiny claws in as she climbed.

"Ouch! I'm not a climbing frame. I bet Dazielle doesn't put up with this kind of behavior." I plucked the feisty kitten off my leg and set her down next to Wiggles. "Entertain her while I finish breakfast."

"Do I have to? She's so annoying. Can't you shut her in the bedroom?"

Phantom squeaked her disapproval and jumped on his back before grabbing hold of one of his ears and giving it a shake.

"She loves you. And I know you like her. Go play away from me, or the next pancake will end up on the floor."

"I have no problem with eating off the floor." Wiggles turned and trotted away, the adorable kitten clinging onto him and growling.

I finished making two pancake stacks and set them on the table. I brought over my mug of coffee then settled in a seat.

Wiggles was already munching on his pancakes from the seat opposite me. Phantom sat beside his plate, looking on with interest as he devoured the food in greedy gulps.

"Let's talk murder while we eat. We need to run over who we've got left and who we've eliminated from the suspect list," I said.

"It's not Hester. We've got witnesses who saw her just before the murder."

"And we know she was covering for Dazielle. Hester took the bloody feather and hid it from me."

"We need to get that back. There could be evidence on it," Wiggles said.

"It'll be too contaminated to be any good to us now," I said. "And we have two options for that feather. Dazielle put it in the drawer after killing Irin, or someone planted it."

"Why would she sneak back to her office and leave that feather there?"

"There's no logic behind it. Lailah suggested it could have been planted, and that's the option I'm going for. It's so unlike Dazielle to leave behind a mess."

"If Dazielle ever killed someone, she'd do it from a distance," Wiggles said. "She wouldn't want to get blood or brains splattered all over her white wings."

I grimaced. "Dazielle would want any murder she committed to be neat and tidy. She'd probably use distance magic."

"Or pay someone else to do it."

I groaned. "What are we talking about? Dazielle didn't kill Irin. It's not her style. None of this makes any sense. The same goes for the bloody angel scythe found in that box in her apartment. Why not dispose of it?"

"Or at least clean it up and put it away in her serial killer display box."

I nodded. "Again, the pattern doesn't fit Dazielle's behavior. If she used the angel scythe, she'd have cleaned it up and tucked it away. She wouldn't have left it filthy and under a blanket for anyone to find."

"Not anyone. Unless they had my superior clue hunting nose, they'd have never found it."

I grinned at him. "Okay, you did a good thing by finding the murder weapon. Moving on from Dazielle. The killer isn't Elyon or Felice. They were together."

"And Lailah saw them." Wiggle chewed on a piece of pancake. "Which leaves us with Gadreel, the abandoned fiancé."

"When I saw him at the wedding, he was already drunk. He was slurring his words and staggering about. He was so wasted, he'd have had trouble walking in a straight line, let alone sneaking up on an angel and neatly cutting off her wings."

"Unless he was faking being drunk," Wiggles said. "He could have put on a show, so everyone simply saw a drunk idiot. When no one was paying attention to him, he snuck into the garden and killed Irin."

"Gadreel was doing a great job of faking being drunk when I talked to him. But he must have been angry about being passed over in favor of Dominic, and right at the last minute. It would have been a shock. Dazielle's family has influence, and he missed out on being a part of that."

"So he killed Irin to ruin Dazielle's wedding?"

"Or maybe he was jealous of Irin's business success and her connections?"

"Or Irin could have wronged Gadreel when they worked together," Wiggles said. "She annoyed him, so he framed Dazielle and got rid of Irin. He removed two problems in one go."

"But how do we prove any of that?" I forked up the last of my pancake and chewed on it.

Wiggles fell off his seat as Phantom pounced on him.

"This murder comes back to love and hate," I said, talking to myself, since the furballs were engaged in a battle to the death as they rolled around the floor. "The attack on Irin was brutal. Slicing off her wings must have been done by someone who truly hated her and knew what losing them would mean. They took away what it meant to be an angel."

Wiggles rolled toward me, Phantom in his mouth. He spat her out and squashed her under his paw. "Gadreel has motives. He hated Dazielle and might have had a problem with Irin."

"We need to find him," I said. "I haven't heard from any of the angels about him coming in for an interview. They should have been able to reach him by now."

"Unless he's done a runner because he felt the net closing in on him." Wiggles ducked as Phantom wriggled out from under his paw and growled at her.

"Gadreel can run, but we'll track him down."

"There is one thing you skirted around when we talked about Dazielle," Wiggles said.

"What's that?"

He trotted along as I collected the breakfast things, ignoring Phantom, who had his tail in her mouth. "Dazielle was really stressed because she was being forced into marrying a moron. She thought she'd gotten away with it when she came up with a plan to fake falling in love with Dominic, but then her mom forced her to marry him."

"So she killed Irin? Why?"

"Dazielle snapped. I always thought her grumpiness would make things end badly."

I shook my head. "Nope. I still don't believe it was her."

"Even though she has no alibi, and the murder weapon was found in her place?"

"Which must have been planted, just like the feather," I said.

"By someone who can walk through walls?" Wiggles said.

I huffed out a breath of frustration. "I still haven't figured out how they got in there and planted the evidence."

"All I'm saying is Dazielle can get really grumpy, but maybe we've never seen her when she's truly angry. I know you've become buddies, and I have nothing against Dazielle, but if everything points to her being the killer, maybe she is."

Phantom hissed at Wiggles and slashed at his nose.

"I'm in agreement with you, Phantom. Dazielle didn't do this." I collected my jacket and put on my boots. "Let's head to Angel Force and see if they've made progress with Gadreel." He was my last hope to get Dazielle in the clear, and I didn't feel all that great that it would pan out the way I wanted.

I just needed a solid confession from him. How hard would that be?

After settling Phantom down with a few toys and a small plate of food, we left the apartment.

I walked into Angel Force and headed to the back storage rooms, where Oriel liked to work. "Morning. Any word on Gadreel coming in for an interview?"

"Hey, Tempest. So far, no luck. I've been over to the hotel twice, and I've left several messages, but he's responded to none of them."

"I told you he'd done a runner," Wiggles said.

"He is still at the hotel, right?" I said. "Tabitha hasn't checked him out?"

"He's still there. I guess I just keep missing him."

"Or he doesn't want to talk to us."

"Because of his guilty conscience," Wiggles said.

"I'll go over there now. I need to see him."

Cassiel marched over. "I've got the results from the angel scythe. There are no prints on it, and it was wiped clean. The blood is a match for Irin. That's the weapon that killed her."

"It's no surprise to hear that, but I was hoping it wasn't connected to the murder." I looked over at the cells. "How's Dazielle doing?"

"She's miserable," Cassiel said. "We're keeping an eye on her."

"Good. Make sure she has everything she needs. I've got someone I need to question. I'll be back to see her soon."

We headed out and walked over to the hotel.

"I have a good feeling about Gadreel," Wiggles said. "He almost trod on me at the wedding, so I knew right away he was a jerk. If Dazielle didn't do it, he's our killer."

"Let's hope he is. Because we're out of options, and I'll have no choice but to charge Dazielle with murder."

We walked into the hotel and over to the reception desk.

Tabitha stood behind the desk. She pushed her glasses up her nose. "Not more hassle? All the angels have been unsettling my guests. Hasn't this murder been dealt with yet?"

"Almost. Is Gadreel in?"

"He has a do not disturb notice on his room."

"Does that mean he's in or not?"

"It means, my guests are free to come and go as they please. He simply wants his privacy."

"I need to speak to him. Which room is he in?"

Tabitha pursed her lips and shook her head. "This place will get a bad reputation if I keep letting witches and angels wander around and quiz my innocent guests."

"What you'll get is a reputation for being helpful in solving a murder. Surely, you want that?"

Tabitha sighed. "He's in room number nine. But be quiet when you speak to him. I have a full house, and I don't want the rest of my guests disturbed."

"So long as Gadreel causes me no problems, we'll be as quiet as mice."

"Fat mice with clogs on," Wiggles whispered.

We headed up the stairs and over to room number nine.

I knocked on the door. Gadreel didn't answer. I knocked again. "Gadreel, this is Tempest Crypt. We need to ask you a few questions about Irin."

Wiggles sniffed at the bottom of the door. "There's someone in there."

I knocked one more time. Gadreel still didn't open the door.

I looked at Wiggles and shrugged. "We tried to do this the quiet way." I grabbed the door handle and used an unlock spell. It didn't work.

"The sneaky angel is using magic to stop us from getting in." I stepped back, conjured a fireball, and blasted it at the door. It smoked, but Gadreel's angel magic held. "Wiggles, I could do with a little extra fire power."

He blasted out a jet of flames, mingling his hellhound power with mine. The door caught light, and a hole burned through the middle, fizzling out the magic barrier preventing us from getting inside.

Wiggles hopped through the hole. I entered behind him and strode into the main room where the bed was.

Gadreel stood on one side of the bed, his wings out, shock written all over his smugly handsome face. "What did you do that for?"

I extinguished the rest of the flames in the room before the whole place went up. "You weren't answering. I figured you needed some encouragement."

"Or you were injured. In case you forgot, there's a killer on the loose, and we wanted to make sure you still had your wings attached to your body," Wiggles said.

I shrugged. "Yeah, that too."

"I... I was busy. And I asked not to be disturbed." Gadreel spread his wings out wider.

"Relax. There's no need to go into angel attack mode. I just need to ask you some questions about Irin's murder."

He glowered at me. "I can't help you with that."

"I think you can. We met at the wedding reception. I don't know if you remember talking to me."

"I talked to lots of people. And I had a lot to drink that night. I don't remember every face or conversation."

"Let me refresh your memory. I'm working with the angels to figure out what happened to Irin."

Gadreel shrugged. "Dazielle killed her. That's what everyone is saying."

"That's yet to be proven. And I know you worked with Irin. What was your relationship like?"

"That's not relevant."

"It could be if you had a bad working relationship. It would give you a motive to kill her."

Gadreel smirked. "You really are clutching at straws if you think I murdered Irin."

He had a point, but I wasn't ready to give up on Dazielle, not while I had this smug angel in front of me. "What was your role in her organization?"

He lifted his wings even higher. When angels stretched out their wings, it was usually a threat display, but all I was getting from Gadreel was panic. His eyes were wide, and every muscle in his body looked so tight that something would snap if he didn't relax. What was he hiding?

"I was her ideas man," he finally said. "Irin worked on the detail, and I was the blue sky thinker. I did the research, talked to the right people, and ran a few viability models. If I got the green light, I handed it over to Irin. She either approved it and fleshed out the detail to make it a reality or told me to try again."

"Did you come up with all the ideas for her business?"

"Irin wouldn't have said that, but it's what she paid me for. I'm what you call an early adopter. I investigate new ideas and concepts from other industries and see if they apply to our business. I've been successful more often than not. Irin valued that kind of thinking."

"Did you come up with the idea to privatize Angel Force?"

His smirk grew. "Irin told everyone it was her idea."

"And that wasn't true?"

"She paid me well for my work. We had a good relationship. I had no plans to rock the boat by speaking out against her. If she wanted to claim that idea was hers, so long as I got a healthy bonus at the end of the year, I wasn't going to say anything to make her look bad."

"It must have annoyed you she was taking the credit for your idea. Were you jealous of her success?"

"When Irin succeeded, I succeeded. I had no complaints." Gadreel inclined his head at what was left of the door. "I've told you everything. You need to go."

"You haven't told me where you were when Irin was murdered," I said.

His wings shook a fraction. "I was slumped in a chair, sleeping it off. I'd had way too much to drink."

"Or maybe you were hunting down Irin because she was eclipsing you, and you got jealous."

"You're being ridiculous. I wouldn't kill Irin."

Gadreel was shaking. Something was up with this angel. "If this murder wasn't about Irin, maybe you wanted to ensure Dazielle had a wedding she'd never forget. After all, she ditched you for Dominic. That must have annoyed you."

"As I said at the bar, I can easily find someone else. I didn't love Dazielle. It was just another business arrangement. The deal got canceled, so I'll need to find myself another partner. It happens all the time in business."

"I thought you didn't remember talking to me when we were at the wedding?"

He jerked his head, and his mouth opened and closed several times. "I remember bits and pieces. Maybe I was angry with Dazielle and her family for pushing me to the side but not angry enough to kill Irin. I'd lost out on a lucrative marriage, so why kill my business associate? I'd already lost one income stream because Dazielle was behaving like an idiot. I wouldn't take away another."

"Try me again with your alibi," I said. "You remembered our conversation at the bar, so you must remember where you were when you heard Irin had been killed."

Gadreel glanced over his shoulder. "I didn't do it."

"So where were you?" I stepped forward, my anger rising, and along with it, a tiny flare from Frank slid up my spine. He'd been quiet this whole time, but he was very interested in Gadreel.

"I... I don't remember. I was drunk and wanted to forget ever meeting Dazielle and her family. I was probably talking to some other guests. Ask around. They'd have seen me."

"I'm asking you." My voice pitched lower as Frank's energy intensified.

Gadreel swallowed loudly. "What's wrong with your eyes?"

"Don't worry about my eyes. Just tell the truth, and I'll leave you alone."

Gadreel backed away. "You don't have to get mean. I promise you, I didn't kill Irin."

"So where were you?"

His shoulders slumped, and his wings lowered.

I glanced behind him to see a table covered with half-opened presents. "Where did you get those?"

"From the wedding reception. You were right. I was angry with Dazielle for passing me over. We would have been a power couple. With her family's influence and my charm, no one would have dared cross us. We'd have had everything, but then she threw it away because of love. I thought she was smarter than that."

"So you stole her wedding gifts?"

Gadreel shrugged. "It's not stealing. These half belong to me. People bought these gifts when they thought I was marrying Dazielle. She changed her mind, and that wasn't my fault. I deserve compensation for missing out on our alliance."

Wiggles snorted a laugh. "So you pinched her presents?"

Gadreel glared at Wiggles as he wriggled under the bed. "I had a few drinks to get up the courage and then snuck into the present room. I was taking out the last pile of gifts when I heard people shouting about a murder."

"So you're a thief but not a killer?" I said.

He pursed his lips. "You can't steal something if it belongs to you."

"Half belongs to you," Wiggles said from under the bed. "What are you going to do with a facial steamer and this weird looking massage wand you've got tucked under here?"

"Those are mine! I'm keeping them. I deserve them. I didn't make a fuss at the wedding. I put on a smile and chatted to everyone and pretended it didn't matter. The presents are my reward."

Wiggles emerged from under the bed and sniffed around the table. "There are three kettles here. Who needs three kettles?"

"Did you steal these things on your own?" I asked.

He shook his head. "I got one of the catering staff to carry out the gifts. He was happy to help."

"What's his name?"

"Rubin, I think. He's a young guy with dark hair and a beard. I gave him a generous tip as a thank you."

"And to buy his silence," I said. "Did he get to pick a gift off the pile as well?"

Gadreel lifted one shoulder. "There were plenty to go around. Dazielle and Dominic won't miss these. And I make no apologies. I wanted what was mine."

I shook my head. "Don't go anywhere while I check your alibi."

His wings rustled. "Or what?"

I growled at him, Frank's energy making me break out in a sweat. "Or you'll regret it. Don't make me hunt you down. You're not to leave Willow Tree Falls until I've checked your alibi and eliminated you from the investigation."

"Or arrested you for murder," Wiggles said.

"Then check it! I've got nothing to hide. I don't even know why you're questioning me. Dazielle killed Irin."

"And you've committed a crime. You'll be charged with theft."

He scowled at me. "I'd like to see you get that charge to stick. No judge would take the case seriously. It was my wedding, so half the gifts are mine."

"We'll see about that. Don't go anywhere. I might want to talk to you again about this little matter of theft." I turned and left the room, hurrying out with Wiggles before I lost control of Frank.

"Gadreel had loads of presents in there," Wiggles said. "I had a look under the bed, and there were a dozen tucked under there, too. It must have taken him ages to sneak out all those gifts."

"Meaning he was busy raiding the present pile and not killing Irin." I scrubbed a hand down my face. "If Gadreel's alibi holds, he can't be the killer."

"And that leaves Dazielle in the frame," Wiggles said.

I nodded. "I'm afraid it does."

Chapter 19

I stepped out of the wedding reception venue, a frown on my face.

Wiggles trotted over. "Did Gadreel lie about his alibi?"

I shook my head. "He didn't. Rubin was reluctant to talk, but when I threatened him with being arrested, he got motivated. Gadreel paid him to load up as many presents as he could and carry them out the back. Gadreel had even started taking them back to the hotel. He isn't our killer."

"Which leaves us with..."

I sighed. "It leaves us with Dazielle."

"Are you going to have her charged?"

I turned and headed toward Angel Force. "I don't want to."

"Maybe she's remembered something useful. Something that points us to another suspect."

I had a bad feeling in my stomach as I walked into Angel Force. I nodded at all the angels, who were busy working, then headed straight to the cells.

Dazielle was in the cell closest to the door. She sat on her cot, her elbows on her knees and her wings wrapped around her.

She glanced up as I approached then shook her head. "I can tell by the look on your face it's bad news."

"I've come to a dead end with the other suspects," I said. "I've discounted your mom, Felice, Elyon, and even your slimy ex-fiancé, who, by the way, stole a load of your wedding gifts at the reception. I found them in his hotel room."

"Why would he do that?"

"Because Gadreel felt you owed him for ditching him on the big day." I pulled up a chair and set it in front of the cell before sitting. "He was trying to hide what he did, but it came tumbling out when we found the gifts."

"He can have them. They're no use to me. Not in here."

I leaned closer to the cell. "Dazielle, look me straight in the eye and tell me you didn't kill Irin."

Her head shot up. "Even you doubt me?"

"I don't want to, but I've eliminated everyone else. It only leaves you."

"And the evidence supports that," she said after a short pause. "Whoever set me up has done a great job. They must really hate me to go to such great lengths."

"Um... I mean, you rub people the wrong way sometimes. You can be surly and abrupt, and you're usually rude to me."

"I'm only rude to you when you step out of line. I figured it would put you off of snooping around in cases that don't concern you."

"I bet you're glad of my snooping now," I said.

"If it weren't for you, I'd have already been charged with Irin's murder." Dazielle sat back on the cot. "How's Phantom?"

"She's a spitfire. She's great fun."

"She likes to be hand fed," Dazielle said. "And she gets a bit gassy after a big meal. I sometimes rub her stomach, which seems to help."

I grinned. "You've totally fallen for that kitten, haven't you?"

"It's not so terrible to have company."

"Phantom is fine. And you'll be back with her soon enough, just as soon as I can find another suspect to grill. Who have I missed?"

The door opened, and Dominic walked in. He gave me a cheery smile and then looked at Dazielle. "I've got good news."

"Have you found a new suspect?" I said.

"Oh, no! It's nothing to do with the murder. But I was speaking to Lailah yesterday. She thinks it's possible we can annul our marriage. After all, we didn't... well, you know, we didn't..." He looked at me, panic in his eyes.

I stifled a grin. "You didn't have a honeymoon night?"

"Yes! That's it."

"I think the steamiest things got between you was that timid kiss in the wedding chapel," I said.

Dominic nodded swiftly. "That's right. Lailah is certain she can arrange for things to be dissolved discreetly. We'll both be free."

"And that's good news?" Dazielle gave a huge sigh. "My mom will be so disappointed in me. All she's ever wanted was to see me on the arm of an eligible angel, doing the social circuits and putting our name out there for everyone to be impressed. Now, I have a failed marriage behind me, and I'm about to be charged with murder. It's like her worst nightmare come true."

"I thought you'd be happy," Dominic said. "I don't exactly want to be a divorced angel. I mean, we could try to make a go of it if you like, but..."

"It's probably for the best if you end things as quickly as possible," I said.

Dominic shot me a grateful look. "I agree."

"Sure. You're right. Thanks for looking into it," Dazielle said. "Besides, you don't want to be associated with a killer. Do what has to be done, and if there's paperwork to sign, I'm happy to sign it. This was never a real marriage."

"I'll get right on that," Dominic said. "And... I'm sorry things didn't work out between us. I mean, I know it wasn't a genuine marriage, but maybe we could have rubbed along together. Although I had always hoped to marry for love one day." Dominic glanced at me, a hopeful look in his eyes.

I shook my head. "I'm not all that interested in marriage myself. You should stay single."

Dazielle chuckled. "Dominic, don't waste your time pining after Tempest. She's not right for you."

"And you'll make someone a great husband one day," I said.

His smile had a wistful tilt to it. "Of course. And I suppose now Rhett's back, you—"

I jerked up in my seat. "What did you just say? Rhett's back in Willow Tree Falls?"

He nodded. "I saw his motorbike this morning. Someone said he arrived last night."

My stomach churned, and I glanced at the door. Why hadn't he come to see me if he was back in the village?

"Is there somewhere you'd rather be, Tempest?" Dazielle said sharply.

I shook my head. "No, you're fine. Let's focus on the murder." Rhett had left me, and I wasn't running back to him just because he'd cruised into the village. Even though a part of me secretly wanted to. He had a lot of making up to do if there was any chance of us rekindling what we had.

"Go if you like," Dazielle said. "There's no point in helping a lost cause."

"You're not a lost cause," I said. "What have we missed? Is there any clue or question in your head that we haven't covered? I need something to stop you from going to trial for murder."

Dazielle and Dominic were quiet for a long time.

"I've got nothing," Dazielle said. "I would have gone after the same people as you. The younger boyfriend, the business partner, and Gadreel are all obvious suspects. Although maybe you'd have gotten to them faster if my mom didn't confess because she thought I was the killer."

"Your mom's actions were wrong, but she did it for the right reason," I said.

"I know. She's been to see me a couple of times. I don't know what to say to her, though. I've ruined everything."

"Not yet, you haven't. I can't do anything about your complicated romantic life, but I'm not giving up on you. I'll keep working on this with Dominic and Lailah." I looked at Dominic. "I haven't seen Lailah this morning. She usually beats me into the office."

"She dropped by first thing and said she had something to do for work, but she'd be back later."

"Lailah probably has another wedding to plan," Wiggles said. "Or a funeral. She could be planning Irin's funeral."

"There's a gloomy thought." I looked back at Dazielle. "Lailah's been useful. You should consider employing her."

Dazielle shifted on her cot. "Lailah always wanted to work for Angel Force when she was younger."

"She enjoys the snooping around and the research. And the higher angels like her. She could be an asset."

"That's not what I meant. We took the same classes at college and even went through the Academy together."

"I didn't know Lailah trained to join Angel Force. What happened? Did she decide a life of law enforcement wasn't for her?"

Dazielle tilted her head from side to side. "Lailah didn't get offered a place because she missed an important exam, so she went into ceremony officiating instead."

I narrowed my eyes. Dazielle wouldn't meet my gaze and looked uncomfortable as she kept squirming around on her cot. "That's a big change of career, especially after going through all the Academy training."

"It was a surprise to everyone."

"And to go from wanting to work for Angel Force to officiating weddings, angel cleansings, and funerals. Did something happen other than the failed exam?"

"Not that I know of. I mean, it was the final exam, so we were all under loads of pressure. Lailah doesn't handle stress well. She must have realized this work would always be high-pressure. It's not for everyone."

"Maybe not. But Lailah was in her element when she helped me. And she suggested useful theories about motives for murder. I could see her working for Angel Force."

"Well, I don't know about any of that. We weren't all that close. She must have just changed her mind." Dazielle looked away. "I'll have a think about other suspects you could question and let you know if I come up with anything useful."

"Not so fast. What are you covering up?"

"It's nothing important, and it was a long time ago. I'd almost forgotten about it."

"What was a long time ago?"

Dazielle sighed. "You must understand, I never had a problem with Lailah when we were in college. But when we got to the Academy, we found out there was a limited number of spaces available for angels who wanted to join Angel Force."

"Go on. You were worried Lailah was a threat to you getting a job?"

"She was great at all the exams and excelled in essay writing. I was panicking. My mom was putting pressure on me to be top of the class, and Lailah was my main competition. It was always the two of us vying for the top spot. And the student who got the highest grade got a fast pass through Angel Force training, a bonus, and an automatic promotion after they'd been in the job for two years. It was too good to miss. I had to be the best."

"Dazielle, what did you do to Lailah, so she lost out on that top spot?"

She ducked her head and plucked at a stray feather. "It's not something I'm proud of, but on the day of the final exam, I might have used a little angel magic so Lailah overslept."

Dominic stared at her with wide eyes. "You made Lailah miss her final exam, so she didn't get into Angel Force?"

"I had no choice! I was freaking out. I had to get that place, or my mom would have disowned me." Dazielle fluttered out her wings. "And I don't know why you're making such a big deal about it. It's not important, and it was ages ago. Lailah is happy. She's got a good job, she's respected, and even the higher angels like her."

"Dazielle! You're kidding me. You ruined her career. It's actually a surprise she hasn't come after you before now."

"Come after me? She hasn't come after me."

I shook my head. "Lailah must be the killer!"

Chapter 20

Dazielle spluttered out a laugh. "It can't be Lailah. She's sweet and helpful. She wouldn't hold a grudge after all this time."

"I disagree. Tell me everything you know about her," I said.

Dazielle glanced at Dominic. "This isn't relevant. You're looking in the wrong place. My... my actions wouldn't have made Lailah do this."

"Tell me anyway," I said. "You went to the Academy together. How close were you?"

"Not that close. We had a friendly rivalry. I only ever paid her attention when I realized she was a threat to me missing out on the top spot in the Academy."

"I'm embarrassed to call you my wife," Dominic said. "You cost Lailah her career."

"You're not the only one who's embarrassed," Dazielle muttered.

I looked up at Dominic in surprise. I'd never heard him so angry.

Dazielle waved a hand in the air. "Lailah can't be the killer."

"Let's pretend she could be. Has she ever done anything to you to make you concerned? Has she ever threatened you or argued with you over losing out on her place at Angel Force?"

"No! Nothing like that. We didn't speak for a while after she left the Academy. That was my doing, not hers, though."

"I'm not surprised. You must have felt guilty about what you did to her," Dominic said.

"I did. And there's no need to rub it in," Dazielle said. "I had a lot of pressure from my family to do well. I couldn't tarnish our reputation. Mom wasn't thrilled about me going into law enforcement, so I had to show her I had a natural flare for crime solving and was the best in the business."

Dominic crossed his arms over his chest. "So you messed with someone else's life to further your own ambitions. You sound just like Irin. And look what happened to her."

"Dominic, why don't you get us some coffees?" I said.

"Happily. My wife's a schemer, and I don't want to be around her another second." He huffed out a breath and then turned and walked away.

I arched a brow at Dazielle. "Oh, dear! You've disappointed your new husband. You won't get a back rub from him now."

She growled at me. "Stop making this worse."

"Dazielle, you have to see how bad this looks. And you haven't learned anything by messing with Lailah. You're still interfering in people's lives."

"I'm not! I fix problems, not cause them."

"Didn't you just force Dominic into marrying you?" Wiggles said.

Dazielle sucked in a breath. "There was no physical force involved. I didn't drag him down the aisle!"

"And you lied to your mom about being in love with Dominic," he said.

"And let's not forget, you offered Dominic his job back, providing he join in with the lies. He loves working here, so you manipulated him." I wagged my finger at her. "You're a bad angel."

"I was young, ambitious, and thoughtless. I wouldn't do it now." Dazielle closed her eyes for a second. "Do you really think Lailah has been holding a grudge all this time?"

"Yes! She failed her final exam and didn't get a chance to fulfill her ambition because of you."

"Lailah has a good career. She seems happy."

"Is being a ceremony officiant as good as working for Angel Force?"

Dazielle pursed her lips. "Some angels don't think so. But they're snobs. I never pay attention to what they think."

"Lailah said she enjoyed this kind of work. I didn't pick up on it, but she must have been alluding to her time at the Academy."

Dazielle groaned. "Most likely. She had a knack for putting everything together and seeing the clues other people missed."

"Which would also give her a gift for framing someone. She'd know which clues to plant and how to misdirect me."

Dazielle's face paled. "Lailah is behind this!"

I nodded. "Now I think about all our conversations, she's been gently nudging me toward you. She even suggested you could be jealous of Irin's relationship with Elyon."

Dazielle snorted a laugh. "I barely know Elyon. I've met him at a few events, but he never said much. He was too busy running around after Irin and trying to keep her happy."

"You weren't ever jealous of Irin's success with men?"

"All I cared about was that she didn't ruin Angel Force. I had no interest in her relationships. She could date a half-demon for all I care, so long as he made her happy."

"It was just another attempt at getting me to see you as a killer. She almost succeeded. And Lailah even suggested the clues we found were planted," I said. "She almost told me the truth but kept back just enough to conceal the fact she was the one planting them."

"Why murder Irin? They had no problems that I'm aware of," Dazielle said.

"To frame you," I said. "This murder has been about getting revenge on you. The business rivalry and the fake love interest were smoke screens. All this time, Lailah's been silently seething because you ruined her career. She saw this as an opportunity to get revenge, ruin your big day, and set you up as a killer. It couldn't have been more perfect."

"There's one problem with this theory," Wiggles said. "Not only do I think Lailah is awesome and not a killer, but she also has an alibi for the time of the murder. She was with Felice and Elyon."

"So they say, but we need to double-check that alibi," I said. "And Lailah was quick enough to encourage them to say they got caught by her at the wedding reception. What if she made them give her an alibi?"

"What did she catch them doing?" Dazielle said.

"They were *together*. You know, arms wrapped around each other in a dark corner, tongues tangling, chests heaving. That kind of together."

"Oh! Irin wouldn't have been happy about that."

"Lailah said she stumbled in on them, but maybe that never happened, and she got them to lie for her."

"They would have wanted her to keep quiet about the affair," Dazielle said. "Elyon was still with Irin at the wedding."

"So Lailah threatened to reveal what they were up to, unless they said they were with her. Elyon seemed shifty when I spoke to him and Felice. That must have been why. He's a bad liar."

"I'm still not sure you're right," Dazielle said. "What I did to Lailah wasn't that bad. It certainly wasn't worth framing me for murder on my wedding day."

"Don't be so sure about that." I hopped from my seat and headed to the door. "Stay right there. I need to talk to Felice and Elyon again."

I raced out of Angel Force with Wiggles and over to the hotel.

"I don't want it to be Lailah," Wiggles said. "She's nice. She's always petting me and feeding me treats. And aren't killers supposed to be horrible to animals?"

"Not this one. It must have been an act."

"You can't fake loving me," Wiggles said. "I'm awesome."

"Okay, maybe she likes you, but Lailah hates Dazielle. I can't believe Dazielle did that to her. She ruined Lailah's career to make a name for herself."

"That's what happens when you have parents who put too much pressure on you," Wiggles said. "That's why I'm glad you're so relaxed with me. I never feel the need to prove my worth."

I dashed into the hotel. "Tabitha! Which rooms are Felice and Elyon staying in?"

She shook her head. "Not again!"

"This is important."

"It's always important when it comes to you poking about in other people's business."

"You could be stopping a killer from being discovered. You don't want that news getting out, do you?"

She gave a dramatic sigh and pointed along the hallway. "They're next to each other, in rooms two and three. Wait! Before you race off, I want a word with you. What happened to the door in room number nine? It's trashed."

"I'll explain another time." I hurried along the hallway.

"I'm sending you the repair bill."

"Send it to Angel Force. I was working under their authority." I reached the first room. I went to knock, but the door was already ajar, so I pushed it open. "Felice? Elyon? It's Tempest." I stopped as soon as

I got inside. The room was a mess. A lamp was smashed, the bedding crumpled, and the pillows were on the floor. But what drew my attention was a smear of blood on one wall.

"This looks bad," Wiggles said. "I smell sweaty angel in here. Their fear is still lingering in the air. And perfume. I smelt that scent on Felice."

I dashed to the next room and knocked on the door. There was no reply.

"Tabitha, unless you want another door with a hole in it, I need you to open room number three," I yelled along the hallway.

She bustled toward me, a scowl on her face. "Keep your voice down. There are other guests here. Why do you need to get in this room?"

"Take a look next door. That'll explain everything."

She walked into the room, and I heard a gasp. She raced back out. There was a key in her hand, which she stuck into the lock. "Whatever is going on?"

"That's what I'm trying to find out." I headed into the room, Tabitha right behind me.

There was no one in there, and a check of the closet and drawers showed they were empty. There were two glasses and an open bottle of brandy on the chest of drawers.

"Is this Elyon's room?" I said.

"That's right." Tabitha looked around with wide eyes, crouching as if she expected to be jumped on at any second.

"Has he checked out?"

"No, he's staying two more days."

"Has another angel been by this morning? Her name is Lailah. She'll have asked to speak to Felice and Elyon."

"I haven't seen any other angels, but I haven't been on the desk the whole time. One of the guests was unwell in the night, so I was helping her. Is Lailah dangerous?"

"She could be. Let me know if she shows up, but I think I'm too late. She's taken what she needed."

"Lailah stole something from the hotel? Did she destroy the room next door?"

"It's likely. And she didn't take things. She grabbed Felice and Elyon." Lailah's plan was unravelling, and it looked like she was trying to cover up her deception by destroying any loose ends.

I headed back into the other room and had a good look around.

Tabitha followed me as I explored. "Tempest, you're worrying me. An out-of-control angel is a dangerous creature. Shouldn't you have back-up?"

I pointed at Wiggles.

Tabitha shook her head. "I meant other angels."

"We'll be fine." There were no clues to suggest where Lailah had gone with Felice and Elyon. But from the mess left behind, Felice hadn't gone willingly. She could be injured or worse.

"Should I lock the main doors and not let anyone in?" Tabitha continued to hover around me. "And what about the other guests? Should I tell them to stay in their rooms in case Lailah attacks them?"

"I doubt she'll come back. You're safe here. Come on, Wiggles." I raced away from the hotel, my pulse pounding.

"Where should we look for Lailah?" he asked.

"If she's hiding Felice and Elyon, it'll be somewhere out of the way."

"The forest?"

I shrugged. "Possibly. If she's in there, it'll take ages to find her."

"Lailah must have more power than we realized if she can subdue two angels on her own."

"Unless she took them one at a time," I said. "Elyon's room wasn't messed up, which suggests he didn't put up a fight." I scanned the streets, looking for any sign of where they might have gone. My head began to ache. It wasn't a typical headache kind of pain, but a pulsing throb from the middle of my forehead.

"Elyon likes a drink. Maybe Lailah got him drunk and led him away somewhere," Wiggles said. "Or she drugged him. She could have slipped something into his drink and then flown off with him while he was unconscious. There was an open bottle of brandy in his room."

"That would work. Lailah visited and pretended she wanted to celebrate the killer being caught. She poured the drinks, mixed in the drugs, and then—" I smacked my forehead. "Of course. Angel wings! Lailah could have flown up to Dazielle's apartment. She didn't need a key, or to be able to walk through walls. She simply waited until Dazielle opened a window, flew up, crept inside, and planted the angel scythe."

Wiggles growled, and smoke billowed out of his nose. "Lailah deceived me. She pretended to be a nice angel, and all the time, she was feeding us lies and hiding the fact she was a killer."

"And Lailah thought she had it all figured out," I said. "But Felice and Elyon must have had second thoughts about covering for her. After all, Irin's dead, so they don't need to hide their relationship anymore."

"They must have panicked when Lailah confronted them at the wedding," Wiggles said. "They didn't want to get in trouble, so they agreed to lie for her."

"But after the dust settled, they realized there was no need. If they'd come to Angel Force and confessed Lailah's alibi was false and she'd forced them to lie, it would have revealed the truth." I looked around. "She could be anywhere. She could even have flown out of the village. What if we're too late?"

Wiggles raised his nose and sniffed. "I'm picking up a faint smell of Lailah but nothing recent."

"If she took Elyon and Felice last night, she's got a big head start on us."

"You don't think she'd kill them, do you?"

My gut clenched. "She might. If they were planning to reveal the truth, she'd need to keep them quiet. Maybe she checked in on them at the hotel to make sure they were leaving, and they told her their plans."

"Where do you dispose of two huge angels?" Wiggles trotted one way and then the other.

"We need to find Lailah and ask that question." I rubbed my forehead and grimaced. It felt like someone had jabbed my skin with a hot poker. My fingers brushed across the higher angel mark. It was warm to the touch, and a spark shot out of it.

Wiggles leaped out of the way before the spark zapped him on the behind. "What was that? Are you okay?"

"I must have my idiot hat on today. I never use this angel mark, but it can help us find Lailah." I touched it. "She's an angel. It should be able to locate her."

Wiggles peered at my forehead. "It's worth a try."

I scooped him into my arms and then pressed firmly against the angel mark. "Find Lailah. Take us to her."

The ground tilted under my feet, and everything went black for a second. I gripped Wiggles tightly, uncertain where we'd end up.

Two blinks later, we arrived in Dazielle's apartment. It only took me a second to get my bearings, and I quickly spotted Lailah. She stood at the table, reading something.

I grinned. *Got you.*

Chapter 21

"Hey! What have you got there?" I said.

Lailah jumped back, and her hand shot to her chest the second she saw me. "Tempest! How did you get in here?" She looked behind me.

I glanced around to see the window open. "A different way than you. What are you doing here?"

"Oh! I... I thought I'd come back and have another look around to see if we missed any evidence."

"What's that on the table?" I set Wiggles down and walked over to her, trying to play it cool.

A nervous smile flicked across her lips. "It's incredible. I just discovered this letter in a drawer. It must have been written by Dazielle. She's confessing everything. Her interest in Elyon, her jealousy of Irin. She even claims that everything Irin touched went wrong. Dazielle had to make sure that didn't happen to Angel Force. She sounds unhinged. Poor Dazielle."

I glanced at the letter. There was no way Dazielle would write that. "That's a handy piece of evidence to uncover, especially since Dazielle's still saying she's innocent. It makes the case against her almost airtight."

Lailah nodded. "She'll have to give up soon. There's too much evidence against her. The feather in her desk, the murder weapon in her apartment, this letter, and her lack of alibi. She must have been feeling guilty, which is why she wrote this. It was a way to unburden her conscience. I expect she hoped it would be found."

"That letter is definitely the sign of a desperate angel," I said. "An angel who must feel everything is falling apart, especially since she worked so hard to hide the truth."

"I agree. I never wanted Dazielle to be the killer, but there's no denying it anymore. She murdered Irin. Dazielle couldn't handle the pressure and snapped. She wanted what Irin had, and when she didn't get it, she lost control." Lailah shook her head. "It's such a pity, especially given the position she holds. And her mom will be so disappointed. I can only imagine what the higher angels will think."

I glanced at Wiggles, who was glaring at Lailah. "It's horrible when an angel loses control. And it must be hard, carrying that kind of hatred and all those vengeful thoughts for such a long time."

"Dazielle will need help," Lailah said. "I'm sure she'll get it. She's done good work for Angel Force. They'll look after her. Maybe her good record will mean she gets a lighter sentence or at least a decent amount of therapy."

"I have no doubt Angel Force will continue to look after Dazielle." I crossed my arms over my chest. "I'm not sure what they'll do with you, though."

Lailah laughed. "Me? Do you think they'll offer me a job? Wouldn't that be fun? We could work together all the time. We make a great team. And I just love Wiggles. I could get my own hellhound, and we could partner up. Would you like a furry friend, Wiggles?"

He snorted. "I've got enough friends."

"Oh dear! Someone got out of the wrong side of the bed today. Has Tempest been working you too hard?"

A flicker of sadness hit me, but I shoved it away. Lailah was a dangerous, out-of-control angel, and she had to be stopped. "I dropped by to see Felice and Elyon this morning, but they weren't at the hotel. Have you spoken to either of them?"

She shook her head. "Can't say I have, but I've been busy clue hunting. Although I heard they were planning on leaving early. Elyon's smitten with Felice, and there was even talk about them eloping. Isn't that romantic?"

"I'm not so sure it is. Didn't you say them getting together so soon was disrespectful? And now they're planning on getting married while Irin's body is still in the mortuary. It's the height of contempt."

Lailah bit her bottom lip. "Oh! Yes, perhaps you're right. I got swept up in the moment. I'd love it if an angel romanced me and promised me the world. Especially one as handsome as Elyon."

"Do you think they've already left Willow Tree Falls?"

"Yes, I'm sure of it. And now I think about it, I saw them as I was coming over here this morning.

I didn't speak to them, but they were carrying their suitcases, so they must have been heading out of the village. I doubt we'll ever see them again. They'll probably set up home in some fabulous angel paradise, just the two of them."

A knot tightened in my stomach. *Had Lailah killed Felice and Elyon?*

"And give up their jobs? Felice sounded almost as ambitious as Irin. You think she'd become an angel of leisure just because she's fallen for Elyon?"

"Elyon said he might get into modelling, didn't he? I'm sure that'll pay for all their needs." A flash of irritation crossed Lailah's face. "Anyway, what shall we do about this letter?"

"Ignore it."

"Why? It's important."

"It's a fake. Lailah, you've been keeping secrets," I said. "And all this time, I thought you were on my side."

Her eyes widened. "I... I am. And I've been helpful."

"Have you? Or have you been distracting me so you could put your plan into action? Was this what you always intended? You played the good, helpful angel, while you secretly framed Dazielle for Irin's murder?"

Lailah jabbed a finger at the letter. "Why are you saying that? This letter explains everything. It's a confession. You have everything you need to charge Dazielle with murder. Why are you suggesting I had anything to do with it?"

"Because Dazielle admitted what she did to you."

Lailah's lips thinned as she pressed them together. "What did she tell you?"

"She told me how you two vied for the top spot at the Academy. You never mentioned that to me. Why didn't you tell me you once wanted to join Angel Force?"

"That was a long time ago. I barely remember any of my training. And all my knowledge is out of date. I didn't mention it because it wasn't relevant."

"You must have been so angry at Dazielle. She made you miss your last exam, and you flunked out of the Academy because of her."

"Is that what she said?"

I nodded. "Dazielle didn't seem to think it was a problem, but I could tell she was embarrassed that her secret was exposed. Have you been holding a grudge all this time?"

"I don't hold grudges. That's not the angel way." Lailah looked at the letter. "Perhaps I was annoyed. But Dazielle's right; it's not a problem. And I have all of this." She spread out her hands.

"You spend your days running around after stressed out people and seeing them live their happiest days. How much happiness does that bring you? Remind me of how many weddings you've officiated."

A muscle twitched in Lailah's jaw. "Dazielle and Dominic's wedding was my six hundred and twelfth. Why is that important?"

"You must get tired, doing the same old ceremony, having to say the same old platitudes, and watching everyone live the high life, while you blend into the background. It must stick in your throat that no one pays you any attention, and they only talk to you because they feel obliged to do so."

"People are always happy to talk to me! And the ceremonies don't get tired. There are always little tweaks that can be made to keep them fresh."

"But think how different your life would have been if you'd joined Angel Force. You'd have been respected. You'd have had a career path. You could have been where Dazielle is. Where does your current job take you? Or is this as far as you go?"

"Maybe this is as far as I want to go. And why are you focused on me? Dazielle is a killer."

"She's not. But you are. You planted the feather in Dazielle's desk, but Hester messed things up when she took it. So you took a risk, snuck in here, and planted the murder weapon. Then you left me and Wiggles to do the rest."

"I planted nothing! Tempest, I thought we were friends."

"So did I, but you've lied to me this whole time."

"Dazielle made a mistake. She must have panicked and stuffed the murder weapon in that box. She didn't have time to dispose of it."

"How did you know it was hidden in a box?" I said. "I never told you where Wiggles found that weapon."

"You did. You told me! I'm certain of it."

I shook my head. "Try again."

She gulped loudly. "Well, someone did. And it was hardly a secret. I have been helping other angels. One of them must have told me."

"Or you knew about it because you put it there."

Lailah's expression hardened. "Has Dazielle put you up to this? I know you're friends."

"No. And she was stunned when I suggested this was all your doing."

Lailah grunted. "I'm surprised she didn't jump on the suggestion. Dazielle enjoys throwing people to the werewolves, so long as it saves her skin."

"Dazielle is on your side."

"That's never going to happen," Lailah mumbled. She sucked in a breath. "Tempest, you must trust me. I had nothing to do with this. This is a big misunderstanding. How about we take the letter to Angel Force and see what everyone has to say about it? Or even go straight to the higher angels? I know they're watching this case with interest."

"I'm more interested in finding out what you've done to Felice and Elyon," I said. "I know one of them is injured. Did you hurt Felice? Did she resist you when you took her?"

Lailah shifted her weight from foot to foot and stepped away from the table. "What have they got to do with this?"

"They gave you an alibi. I thought you were a bit pushy when we met them. You wanted it made clear you were with them when Irin's body was discovered, so you wouldn't be suspected."

"I wasn't pushy. I'm always pleasant." Color rose in her cheeks. "Those angels are deceivers. They hid their affair from Irin. Who knows what they'll try next?"

"Are you thinking about framing them for something, too?"

"Tempest! No! Stop saying that." Lailah clamped a hand against her ear.

"Or maybe they won't be able to do anything, if you killed them."

There was a thump from the bedroom, and I tensed and spun toward the door.

Lailah raced over and stood in front of it. "You should go. Take that letter to Angel Force. You don't want the evidence contaminated."

"That fake letter isn't relevant to the investigation." I stalked toward her, anger simmering through me. I liked Lailah, and I'd trusted her. It hurt to be betrayed. "What have you got hiding in that room? Or should I say, who?"

"Nothing. It must be Dazielle's kitten. It's a feisty little thing."

"It can't be Phantom. She's staying with us," Wiggles said.

My gaze went to Lailah's wrist. "That's where you got the scratches. When you snuck in here and planted the murder weapon, Phantom didn't like it. She was on to you, so she attacked."

Lailah's bottom lip wobbled. "I wish I'd never helped you. Everyone said to be careful around you because of your demon, but I gave you the benefit of the doubt."

"You shouldn't have bothered. And you need to be very careful about your next move."

"Get out of here!" Lailah's wings flared out. "Charge Dazielle with murder. She deserves it. She's a hateful angel."

"I'm not charging an innocent angel for the crime you committed," I said.

There was another thump, and I heard a muffled moan. "Have you got Felice and Elyon in the bedroom?"

"No! They've left the village."

"How about you let me check that room, just to make sure no one snuck in? We don't want any more evidence being planted." I tried to shove past Lailah, but she pushed me back.

"You don't want to make Tempest mad," Wiggles said. "Frank likes to fight angels."

Lailah tilted her head. "Who's Frank?"

"My demon," I said. "Get out of my way and let me speak to Felice and Elyon. I need to make sure they're okay, and then I need to check your alibi with them."

Lailah pushed me again. "They'll only tell you the same thing. We were together when Irin died."

"They won't. That's why you took them. Did they tell you they were planning on revealing the truth?"

"Of course not!" Lailah swiped a wing at me when I tried to dodge past her, skimming it over my head and making me stagger back.

"Felice and Elyon decided not to cover for you. Irin's dead, so they don't need to keep their affair quiet. There's no reason to give you a fake alibi."

Lailah scowled at me. "If they change their story now, they'll be considered unreliable. They might even be charged with perverting the course of justice."

"I thought you didn't remember any of your Academy training."

Her hands clenched into fists. "They're rotten angels, and no one will believe them. And I'll make sure everyone knows they were having an affair. Their reputations will be in ruins. And if they dared go before a jury, they'd be laughed out of the room."

"If you believe they're so unreliable, it won't be a problem if I speak to them," I said.

Lailah shoved me back again. "Stay away from this room."

Frank's energy flared up my spine. I growled at Lailah, and my throat burned. "Push me one more time, and I'll make sure Frank gets to know you very well. He doesn't think much of angels, and it's been a while since he's had one to play with."

Lailah's tongue traced across her lips. "Why have your eyes changed color? What's... what's wrong with you?"

"Nothing's wrong with her. Tempest is awesome. Frank, not so much. You'd better let her past, or you'll get to meet him," Wiggles said.

I forced Frank back. He was only lurking in the background, more curious about what was going on than interested in taking down this angel.

But his shady energy seemed to have an effect, because Lailah stepped away from the door. "This won't make any difference. And I'll report the confession letter to the higher angels. The evidence against Dazielle is still overwhelming. She won't get away with what she's done."

"You mean to you? You wanted revenge for what happened to you." I headed to the bedroom door.

Lailah's eyes filled with tears. "She ruined my life."

"And it's only going to get worse when I tell the higher angels how you misdirected me. You lied about Dazielle's interest in Elyon to send me along the wrong path. You planted evidence, and you wrote that letter. Plus you forced two angels to lie, so you had an alibi."

"No! Don't do that. I... I have the higher angels' respect. They believe in me. They like me and recognize my value. You can't take that away."

I rested my hand on the doorknob. "That's what you want more than anything, isn't it? You want people to value you. You want people to see the work you do as important. As important as Dazielle's work in Angel Force."

Lailah shuffled away. "She had it coming to her."

I lifted a finger. "Hold that confession for a minute. Wiggles, guard Lailah. If she moves, bite her." I shoved open the bedroom door and found Felice and Elyon trussed together and rolling around on the floor.

I yanked the binding off Elyon's mouth. "Are you hurt?"

"I'm okay. A bit woozy. I think I was drugged. One minute, I was talking to Lailah, and the next, I woke up here. Check on Felice. She's not so good."

I loosened the bindings so they could both sit up, the magic on the rope stinging my fingers, and did a quick examination of Felice's injuries. She had a nasty cut on her forehead, and one wing drooped at an unnatural angle.

"It was Lailah," she gasped out. "That nice angel who conducted the wedding ceremony. She burst into my room and attacked me."

"And she's right outside," I said. "But don't worry. Lailah won't hurt you. Elyon, take care of Felice. I'll be right back."

I returned to the living room to find Lailah staring at Wiggles. She hadn't moved an inch.

"Do you want to explain why you had Felice and Elyon tied up in Dazielle's bedroom?"

She slumped onto the couch but said nothing.

"Lailah, the game is up. This was all you, wasn't it?"

She let out a long sigh. "I had to take them. They were going to spoil everything, and I was so close to getting it right. I wouldn't have killed them. I just wanted to talk to them and explain everything. They'd have kept quiet once they knew how awful Dazielle really was."

I glanced at Wiggles and raised my eyebrows before sitting opposite Lailah. "You killed Irin to frame Dazielle?"

Lailah dropped her head into her hands. "I couldn't do it anymore. I hate weddings. They make me sick to my stomach. All the fake happiness, ridiculous expense, and the guests forced to buy extravagant gifts for people they couldn't care less about then act like they're happy. It's rubbish. It means nothing."

"Not every marriage is like that."

"It is for most angels. And they're forced to stay together and form alliances because of centuries of petty squabbles that could be resolved if any of them had a decent brain." She glanced up at me. "You know, I hesitated in going through with this when Dazielle decided she was marrying Dominic instead of Gadreel. I wondered if she had changed."

"You've lost me."

"Dazielle and Gadreel's marriage wasn't a marriage of love. It was just another business arrangement to make their families powerful so they could dominate other angels. That's not how angel society operates. At least, it didn't used to be. Now, we have these new families rising and claiming to be better than everyone else."

"And then I revealed to you that Dazielle didn't love Dominic. They were never supposed to get married."

"It was too late by then. And I'd come too far to back out. Irin was dead, but I was feeling guilty about what I'd done. That guilt vanished when you told me what Dazielle had set up to deceive her family. It served her right she had to marry Dominic."

Lailah continued, "And it's typical of Dazielle to use someone else to avoid a difficult situation."

"All this scheming because of a job? Why didn't you try another career?" Wiggles said.

"I couldn't! Angels laugh at me behind my back, and they think the work I do is a joke. I wouldn't be taken seriously if I tried something different. I'm stuck and all because of Dazielle."

"I didn't hear anyone say anything bad about you at the wedding," I said. "People like you. The higher angels clearly respect you."

"They won't when they learn you're a killer," Wiggles said.

"The angels wouldn't say anything to give themselves a bad reputation, but I know the truth. They see me as less of a supernatural. They all know this wasn't my first career choice. It was all because of Dazielle that I ended up here. She hates to be beaten at anything. Have you noticed how competitive she is? And she always has to be right."

"Um... maybe once or twice," I said.

"I was better than her at the Academy. And I knew I'd get that top spot and the benefits that came with it. I've never forgiven her for messing up my final exam."

"Why didn't you re-sit the exam?" Wiggles said. "I mean, it's a grade on a piece of paper. How important could that be?"

"Extremely important. If you fail to turn up for an exam and don't have a valid reason for not being there, you're judged for the rest of your career. I could have waited a year and re-taken the exam, but my absence was put on my permanent record. I didn't stand a chance."

"Lailah, you're a smart angel. You could have found a way to show you were better than that," I said.

"Don't think I didn't try, but nothing worked, so I became a ceremony officiant. To begin with, I tried to make it something more and focused on helping angels and making them happy, but I got jaded fast. The ceremonies are a joke, and the angels who arrange them are even more ridiculous. I had to change things."

"So you picked Irin as the victim because you knew about her disagreements with Dazielle."

"It was so perfect. Everything fell into my lap. The opportunity to officiate the wedding. Irin being there, swanning around like she owned the place. The fact the higher angels were concerned about

Dazielle and her fights with Irin. The pieces slotted together like the most perfect puzzle. I couldn't ignore my opportunity to ruin Dazielle and take away everything she didn't deserve."

"So you played nice until everyone's attention was off you. Then how did you get Irin outside to kill her?" I said.

"I did nothing special to make that happen. I just kept track of what she was doing. Irin kept slipping outside to send messages. She had one of those expensive mobile snow globes that sends messages anywhere."

"You just waited until no one was watching and then killed her?"

"When there was a noisy song playing, and the dance floor was crowded, I followed Irin out with the angel scythe tucked under my wings. Irin didn't even hear me coming. And it was so quick, just a single slice and a blast of angel fire to knock her down. I never expected the scythe to work that well." Lailah glanced at the box she'd placed the murder weapon in.

A gasp from the bedroom door had me turning. Felice stood there, supported by Elyon.

"Don't pass judgment on me," Lailah said, a sneer on her face. "You two have been cavorting behind Irin's back for months. You should be ashamed of yourselves."

"You killed Irin?" Felice said.

"That's why Lailah attacked you," I said. "Were you coming to Angel Force to tell the truth about that night at the wedding reception?"

Elyon glanced at Felice then nodded. "We'd talked it over and decided it was the right thing to do."

"Even if we got in trouble, we didn't want to live with a lie," Felice said.

"You wouldn't know the truth if it was painted in glitter and displayed too much cleavage." Lailah gestured at Felice's disheveled appearance and the pink bra strap on display.

"Go on, Felice," I said.

She swiftly adjusted her blouse. "I thought nothing of it at first when Lailah came over to us after Irin was killed. She casually mentioned seeing us together and made a joke about it."

"I said Lailah was mistaken," Elyon said.

Felice's cheeks flushed. "We had been together, and I was embarrassed at being caught. But Lailah didn't come in the room when we were... getting to know each other."

"I did. Your memory is muddled because you were drunk," Lailah said.

Felice pushed back her shoulders. "I'd had a few drinks, but my memory is perfect." She looked at me. "Then Lailah insisted we say we were together when we heard about Irin."

"That's when she threatened to reveal our affair to everyone if we didn't do it," Elyon said.

"So we played along. But it wasn't true," Felice said.

Lailah shrugged, an expression of deep disapproval on her face. "I'll make sure everyone knows about you two. You're ruined."

"No, you won't," I said. "Because we're going to Angel Force, so you can confess to Irin's murder. And Felice and Elyon, you need to make new statements."

Elyon's face paled. "Will people find out what we were doing at the wedding?"

"We'll be as discreet as we can," I said. "But your statements are important in making sure Lailah is charged."

"Of course," Felice said. "And Lailah even threatened us when she came to the hotel. When I didn't agree to stay quiet, she said she'd taken Elyon and would kill him. I panicked and hit her, which is how I got this." She touched the wound on her head.

"It looks like we're adding kidnap, assault, attempted murder, and lying to a friendly hellhound to Lailah's list of crimes," Wiggles said.

Lailah glared at him.

"And I didn't understand what Lailah meant when we were fighting, but she said we had to be silenced so justice could be done," Felice said.

"I know what she meant. And justice is about to be done." I gestured Lailah to stand. I wasn't happy about being deceived. I'd trusted her, and she'd let me down. "You're under arrest for murder."

Chapter 22

"Two double stuffed crusts with an extra-large side order of garlic bread, and my magic dough balls with melting middles." Tate placed our huge order on the table in Mystic Mushroom and grinned at me before walking back behind the counter.

I grabbed my first slice and then pushed the pizza over to Dazielle and Dominic.

Dominic picked up a slice and took a huge bite.

Dazielle took a small piece of garlic bread and sniffed it. "I won't need to worry about the vampires if I eat this."

"Stop complaining and get stuck in. This is your celebratory meal. You're no longer a murder suspect. You've been free from the cells for two whole days. Doesn't it feel good to no longer have a target on your back?"

Dazielle arched her eyebrows and nodded. "It took you long enough to figure out what really happened. Although I still can't believe Lailah hated me that much."

"Believe it. She must have been plotting your downfall for a long time. She said the fates aligned, and she had no choice but to frame you for Irin's murder."

"She had a choice," Dazielle muttered.

"Just like you had a choice when you messed up her final exam."

"That was... different."

"Raise your hand if you think Dazielle did a bad thing." I whipped up my hand. Wiggles' paw appeared over the edge of the table, and even Dominic slowly raised a hand.

Dazielle winced. "I didn't realize how badly it affected her. I'll speak to the higher angels and see if we can't get her some help. Maybe a reduced sentence or get her sent to a lower security prison. I can't do much about the time she'll serve behind bars, though."

"It's probably best if the place she goes isn't too low security. Lailah planned to kill Felice and Elyon because they were going to reveal her fake alibi. I think she's a little unhinged."

"She has been forced to hold over six hundred weddings. You'd go crazy being surrounded by so many feathers." Wiggles ducked back under the table with a large chunk of garlic bread in his mouth.

"I'll think about what I can do for her." Dazielle bit into the garlic bread then smiled. "This isn't bad."

"Tate's garlic bread is the best," I said.

We enjoyed a few moments of relaxed silence as we ate pizza.

Dominic took another slice and let out a contented sigh.

"How are you doing?" I asked him.

He gave me one of his big, sunny grins. "I'm happy I've got my job back."

"It's only on a probationary period," Dazielle said.

I shook my head. "No! You take Dominic back for good. You have to stay with each other through the good times and the bad. Isn't that what your vows said?"

Dazielle glowered at me. "You aren't funny."

I touched Dominic's hand. "Are you happy to have such a beautiful new bride?"

He gulped down his mouthful of pizza and glanced at Dazielle. "We're getting the marriage annulled. We've been to see the higher angels. It took us a while to convince them, and I'm not sure they understood what was going on, but they agreed our union doesn't work."

I cocked my head. "I just heard thousands of women's hearts mending in the hope you'll date them now you're single again."

"There you are."

I jerked upright as Hester's cool voice came from behind me. I turned and pushed out a chair. "Join us."

Hester stared at the table of goodies and grimaced. "I never eat pizza. Neither does Dazielle."

Dazielle set down her garlic bread. "Mom! I've been meaning to come and see you."

Hester took the seat I'd pushed out. "And I've been meaning to visit you. We have some talking to do."

Dazielle glanced at Dominic. "You've heard the news about us?"

Hester shook her head. "I'm here to talk about almost pushing you into an unhappy marriage." She reached over and took hold of Dazielle's hand. "I wish you'd spoken to me about how unhappy you were about your match with Gadreel. We'd have worked something out."

"Oh! Really? I figured nothing would change your mind."

"I only want the best for you." Hester smiled. "What news were you referring to? It's too soon to hope for the patter of tiny angel feet."

"Um... it's not important." Dazielle ducked her head.

I kicked her under the table. She couldn't hide the fact her marriage to Dominic was a sham for much longer.

Hester smoothed her hands over her white silk scarf and patted Dominic's cheek. "Everything worked out in the end, since you met this charming angel. I hope you make each other very happy."

Dominic flushed and bit into his pizza, not meeting Hester's gaze.

Hester sighed. "I sometimes forget that marriage is more than an alliance or a useful arrangement. My own marriage... well, we're not here to discuss that."

Dazielle bit her lip and looked at me.

I shook my head and grinned. "You'll have to deal with this all on your own."

"What's to deal with?" Hester said. "Irin's killer has been found, and Dazielle and Dominic are in love. It's a happy ending all around."

"Mom, about that." Dazielle stood and caught hold of Hester's arm. "There's something I need to tell you. Let's take a walk."

Hester stood. "I don't mind what you have to tell me. So long as you're happy."

Dazielle looked at me again. "I will be. I've just got a few loose ends to sort out." They walked out of the pizza parlor.

I chuckled and shook my head. "Dazielle is in so much trouble. I hope she's learned that keeping secrets from your family is always a bad thing."

"Angel families are complicated," Dominic said.

"All families are complicated. You can be a witch, a werewolf, or a vampire, and you'll still have issues with your relatives."

Dominic wiped his fingers on a paper napkin. "All this marriage business has made me think about having my own family. I mean, not children, at least not right away. But maybe find a nice girl to settle down with, get a place together, and enjoy life. What do you think about that?"

"That sounds good to me. Whatever makes you happy." I pulled cheese off my pizza and ate it.

"I meant, how about you and me trying the whole settling down thing?" Dominic's intense blue gaze was fixed on me.

"Oh, Dominic, no! You're an adorable guy, but you're not my sweetheart."

"I could be. I'm a nice guy. I'd always try to make you happy." He reached for my hand. "I'd even buy a motorbike and a leather jacket if that's what you like."

"No! I mean, I like those things, but don't change who you are because of me. That'll only make you miserable. You'll make some woman so ridiculously happy, but it won't be me."

"Is it because I'm blond? I could always dye my hair."

"Stop! You're perfect just the way you are."

He sighed. "But I'm not your kind of perfect?"

The door to the pizza parlor slammed open. Aurora raced in, and close behind her was Zandra.

"We've been looking for you. Come with us," Aurora said. She waved at Dominic and then grabbed a slice of pizza.

"I'm eating. So unless Cloven Hoof is burning down or the demon prison has exploded, I'm going exactly nowhere." I took a huge bite of pizza.

Zandra lifted a slice and inspected it. "I told you to be cool, idiot."

I glanced at my sisters. "Are you two friends, now?"

"Nope," Zandra said. "Blondie is still too loud for me. I get a headache if we spend more than five minutes together."

"We're not enemies." Aurora shot Zandra a filthy look.

"That's a good start. What forced you to talk to each other?"

"We decided, over my homemade chocolate torte, that you needed some fun after dealing with all that horrible murder business," Aurora said. "And we've got just the right fun for you. You're going to love it."

"If it doesn't involve pizza and putting my feet up on the couch for the rest of the evening, I'm not interested."

"I told you this was a waste of time," Zandra said.

Aurora bounced on her toes. "But this will make her happy."

I finished my slice of pizza. "What have you got planned?"

"It's Rhett. He's back." Aurora grinned at me.

I shrugged, pretending not to notice my heart speed up. "I already know that. Dominic told me."

"Aren't you excited? He's here in the village!" Aurora shook me by the shoulder.

"So what? He hasn't come to see me. It shows he's not interested."

"There are other options available, if Rhett's not the guy for you," Dominic whispered.

I smiled at him and shook my head.

"Don't be so stubborn," Aurora said. "We all know you love Rhett. And you could have gone to visit him."

"I've been busy solving a murder," I said. "That was more important than my messed up love life with a guy who's not into me anymore."

Aurora swatted me on the back of the head. "Sometimes, I wish I had no sisters, instead of these pig-headed ones who make trouble for themselves."

"Be careful throwing out wishes like that. You are married to a jinn." I rubbed the back of my head. "Besides, what I said is true. Rhett's been back for days, but he's not dropped by once. He hasn't been to Cloven Hoof or my apartment. I get it. We've both moved on."

"Neither of you have moved on," Aurora said. "And Rhett's been busy making plans for both of you. Plans you're going to love."

My stomach lurched, and I eyed her carefully. "What kind of plans are we talking about?"

"If you get off your behind and follow us, you'll see."

"You're making a big deal out of this," Zandra said. "It's just a guy."

"But it's Tempest's guy. And Rhett makes her happy," Dominic said, a glum expression on his face as he stuffed an entire slice of pizza into his mouth.

I patted his hand. "Enjoy the food. I'll catch up with you tomorrow."

He nodded and waved me away.

Aurora grabbed my arm and tugged me out of the pizza parlor, Zandra and Wiggles strolling along behind us. "I've been speaking to Rhett for ages, and I know he's sorry for leaving without saying goodbye."

"What have you been speaking about?"

"You'll see." She giggled then turned and gestured at Zandra. "Hurry."

Zandra groaned. "You need to stop being so irritating."

"And you need to stop playing it so cool. Everyone knows you're excited about this, too." Aurora reached over and grabbed Zandra's arm.

A bolt of what felt like electricity surged through me. I jerked away at the same time as Aurora squeaked and Zandra yelped.

I looked down at my tingling arm. "What the heck was that? What did you just do to us?"

Aurora's hair stood up around her head in a fluffy halo. "I have no idea. That wasn't my magic. Zandra, was that you? Did you zap us with one of your weird spells?"

Zandra was rubbing her arm. "That didn't come from me. Whatever it was, it had power. I'm tingling all over. I feel... odd."

I shook out my arm. "Me, too." I looked around, but there was no one else anywhere near us. "Wiggles, that wasn't you, was it?"

"Not guilty," he said.

I flexed my fingers as the tingling faded, and I was left with a slight buzzing in my ears. "Let's get out of here. I don't want that to happen again. Where am I meeting Rhett?"

"We're going to Cloven Hoof," Aurora said. "He's waiting for you."

"I hope he's not expecting me to take him back without some serious groveling from his side," I said. "Rhett has some explaining to do."

"That's right," Zandra said. "You shouldn't let a guy stamp all over your heart, throw it away, and then expect you to give it back to him the next time he's ready for you."

"You two are so cynical with matters of the heart! Rhett would never do that to Tempest."

"Err... he stamped on my heart a bit," I said.

"I told you," Zandra said, still rubbing her arm.

"Rhett's different. And like I said, he's been making plans."

"You're making me nervous with all this talk about plans. Rhett lives in the moment. That's what I like about him. There's never any pressure from him to meet relationship goals."

Aurora giggled. "You're going to be so happy."

We reached the doors of the club, and I stopped. "You haven't forced him to propose, have you? That's not what I want. I don't like grand gestures."

"No! It's so much better than that. Well, I would love to be your bridesmaid, but I'm sure that'll come in the future." Aurora grinned at me and pulled open the doors.

I walked in somewhat reluctantly. Rhett stood at the bar, a drink beside him. He turned as I walked in, and my stomach fluttered. I wish he didn't have that effect on me, but I'd always had a huge weakness for this gorgeous warlock.

"We'll leave you to it. Our job is done." Aurora leaned closer to me. "Listen to what Rhett has to say. You won't regret it. And don't be too stubborn."

"You can be as stubborn as you like," Zandra said. "Your club, your rules."

I sucked in a breath. "My heart, my rules." I watched them go and then turned back to Rhett.

He'd moved toward me, and his expression showed he was almost as nervous as me.

"Long-time no see," I said. "What trouble have you been getting into?"

His smile was tentative. "No trouble at all. Hey, Wiggles."

"Hey, jerk."

Rhett chuckled. "I guess I deserve that."

"I'll be in the kitchen. Just yell if you need me to bite anyone." Wiggles growled at Rhett then stalked away.

"I've... been making plans," Rhett said.

"So Aurora told me. Am I supposed to be interested in those plans?" I sidled up to the bar, and Rhett followed me.

"I get that you're angry, but I needed time away. Things got a bit intense, and I didn't want to mess things up between us. Every time we talked, I kept making things worse."

"You've been gone for ages." I nodded at Merrie as she watched us from a distance. "Maybe I've got a new guy."

Rhett's eyes narrowed. "Have you? Has that angel finally worn you down and you've agreed to go on a date with him?"

"If Dominic has, you'd have nothing to complain about. And don't pick on him. He's a great guy."

Rhett huffed out a breath. "Are you dating someone else? Aurora said nothing about that."

"You can't blame me if I have found someone new. You walked out on me."

He ran a hand through his hair. "I knew things had to change. My gang was taking up too much of my time, and you were unhappy."

"I never said that."

"You didn't have to. We were fighting too much, and I was torn in two different directions. The gang expected me to be a certain way, and you needed me to be someone else."

"No! I just expected you to be you. If the person you are doesn't fit in my life, then it was the right thing to do to walk away. I just wish you'd talked to me before you did. Everything was left in the air. I didn't even know if we were still a couple."

"And I was an idiot for leaving things that way. But hear me out before you decide it's too late for us."

I glanced at him. "I didn't say it was too late for us."

"So... there's hope?"

"There's a small hope. It's about the size of a mouse heart." I turned to face him. "What do you need to tell me?"

Rhett drew in a deep breath and let it out slowly. "This is important to me. I hope it will be to you, too."

"I'm listening."

"I've left the gang."

My mouth fell open. "Why did you do that? The gang is your life. Did you have a fight? They didn't kick you out, did they?"

"No, it's nothing like that. And the gang isn't my life, not anymore. I found something much more important. And I want all in with my beautiful witch-angel-demon girlfriend." He reached up and smoothed his thumb across my forehead.

I was too surprised to say anything for a full minute. "Rhett, you didn't have to do that. Not for me."

"I wanted to. And I've done it. I can't let the gang come between us. So, I went away, found them a new leader and a new place to set up base, and I've been working on expanding my sculpture business. I've already got enough commissions to keep me busy for months. I'm going completely legit."

I frowned at him. "That will make you happy? That's enough for you?"

"I want you to be happy, and the gang was getting in our way. You're the most important person to me." He cupped the back of my neck and drew me closer. "I should have handled things better, but I decided to act and show you how serious I was."

"You should have talked this through with me."

"I was done talking. I sorted the gang, got the business rolling, and then came back to see if you'd still have me."

I shook my head. "What if I don't want you? You've done all this for nothing."

Rhett dropped his hand from the back of my neck. "Has it all been for nothing? Am I too late?"

I wanted to be an ice queen and act like I didn't care, but Rhett had a big place in my heart, and he'd sacrificed a huge amount to be with me. It was a little awesome but also a lot terrifying.

"Tempest, will you—"

"Don't you dare propose," I said.

"No, I wasn't going to propose." He grinned. "I was going to ask if you'd be my girl again."

I let out a sigh. "Good. Because I've had enough of weddings to last me a long time."

"I've been hearing about the angel wedding and the murder. I'd love to hear more, if you've got the time to give me." Rhett caught hold of my hand. "I messed up, but I'll be better."

I took a few seconds to process everything he'd told me. "I'll give you some time, but let's take this slow. No labels, no promises. We'll just see how things go."

His grin made my heart melt. "I can handle that. And I figured if we ever got married, you'd decide when and where. You'd probably even make the proposal."

"Would you have a problem with that?"

Rhett's grin turned into a full, breathtaking smile. "Never. And of course, I'd be happy to accept."

I bit my lip, my gaze running over him. I'd missed Rhett so much, but it wouldn't be as simple as letting him step back into my life and everything be normal.

He raised a hand, his smile slipping. "I know we've got a lot to sort out. But I'm back now, and I'm going nowhere."

"Neither am I. Why don't we grab a drink and let's talk some more?" I beckoned Merrie over, and she poured out two large lemon drops.

It was strange but also comforting that Rhett was back. Things would be different between us, but maybe that wasn't such a bad thing.

I raised my glass. "Welcome back. Why don't I tell you about how Dazielle and Dominic accidentally got married to each other?"

Rhett chinked his glass against mine. "I can think of nothing I'd like more. It's great to be home."

About Author

K.E. O'Connor (Karen) is a cozy mystery author living in the beautiful British countryside. She loves all things mystery, animals, and cake. When she's not writing about mysteries, murder, and treats, she volunteers at a local animal sanctuary, reads a ton of books, binge-watches mystery series, and dreams about living somewhere warmer.

To stay in touch with the fun mysteries:

Newsletter:
www.subscribepage.com/cozymysteries

Website:
www.keoconnor.com

Facebook:
www.facebook.com/keoconnorauthor

Also By

Luck of the Witch
Hell of a Witch
Revenge of the Witch
Curse of the Witch
Son of a Witch
Framing of the Witch
Trickery of the Witch
Wishes of the Witch
Harmony of the Witch
Remedy of the Witch
Gift of the Witch
Toil of the Witch
Jinxing of the Witch
Craving of the Witch
Union of the Witch
Chaos of the Witch
Sleighing of the Witch

If you enjoyed

Union of the Witch

turn the page to read an extract from the next Crypt
Witch Mystery

CHAOS OF THE WITCH

Chapter 1

I shook out my fingers as sweat beaded on my brow. I flicked the cleaning spell across the floor of my bar, Cloven Hoof. It didn't work, and this was the fifth time I'd tried casting magic. I could usually do this spell in my sleep.

"Is this your doing, Frank?" I marched across the sticky dance floor, where dozens of drinks had been spilled following last night's revelry. "Don't think you'll get away with messing with my magic."

Frank, my resident demon, barely stirred as I continued to hiss out threats. He'd been like that for months. There was a time, not so long ago, when I'd been worried I was losing control of him, but things had changed, and I had no clue why. He'd barely troubled me for months. But recently, I'd been having difficulty getting my magic to work. It had to be because of Frank's meddling.

I stood on the opposite side of the dance floor. Maybe this blip was because we were close to celebrating an important anniversary for the demon prison. We held an anniversary party every year, but this felt different because we had a thousand years of demon trapping to commemorate.

That could be the problem. The demons were grumpy, and their negative vibes were upsetting my magic.

After three more failed attempts at the cleaning spell, I let out a huff and stomped to the bar. No, this had to be Frank's doing. And he was only giving me the silent treatment because it bugged me. I didn't like him butting in on my life, but I got worried when he was too quiet. It meant he was plotting something. And when a demon plots, you know it's never going to be about candy floss and unicorns.

Merrie Noble strolled along the other side of the bar and set a mug of hot chocolate in front of me. "Still no luck with the cleaning spell?"

"Nope. I can't get it to take. I must be having an off day." Although it had been more like an off few weeks.

"We all get them. I sometimes find my magic plays up around the full moon."

"Have you got werewolf in your family tree?"

She wrinkled her nose. "I don't think so. And I never get furry and start howling, but the lunar cycle unsettles my powers. I make sure I don't plan any complicated spells around that time."

"The moon has never troubled me. It must be something else."

"I'll deal with the cleaning." Merrie nudged my mug closer. "You enjoy your hot chocolate."

I could always rely on her to ensure the club ran smoothly. She was the best bar manager a witch could want.

Ten minutes later, and after a delicious mug of hot chocolate, the place was spotless thanks to Merrie's magic, and I felt less grumpy.

"I love that look on you." She went back behind the bar and began stacking glasses.

I glanced down at my usual outfit of jeans and a long-sleeved T-shirt. "You've seen these jeans about a thousand times."

"Your hair. The blonde stripe."

I grabbed a handful of my long, dark hair and pulled it in front of me. Sure enough, there was a blonde stripe running down one side. "Huh! How did that get there?"

Merrie walked over and studied my new color. "I figured you did it to yourself. It looks good."

I conjured a color change spell and swiped it down the blonde. It didn't budge. I tried several more times, but the color remained.

"You really are having trouble with your magic. Do you want me to have a go?"

"Sure. I don't think I can pull off the blonde look, so this needs to go."

"I like it. Are you sure you want it gone?"

"Yep. Do it."

Merrie stroked a hand over the stripe in my hair. She tilted her head. "That's weird. It didn't work. It must be a strong spell."

I pulled my hair off my face and tied it in a messy bun out of the way. "I'll figure it out later. We've got too much on our plate right now for me to waste time altering my hair."

The door leading to the kitchen was shoved open, and Wiggles, my adorably smelly hellhound, trotted out chewing on something.

"What have you stolen from the kitchen?" I said.

He swallowed and blinked his red eyes at me. "Nothing. Chef was making samples for the party and needed someone to try them out."

"Sure he did. But you've hardly got a discerning palate. Your nose is always stuck in the trash."

"My palate is very refined." Wiggles belched. "And the party food is excellent. I loved the rare beef canapes with mustard relish."

"Do you like Tempest's new hair color?" Merrie said. "Did you sneak in the stripe when she was sleeping?"

Wiggles cocked his head and looked me over. "I don't see any difference."

"Forget about it." I glanced at the main doors of the club. "There's still no sign of the decorations for the party. I'm sure Mom said she was having them delivered here today."

"Oh! I got a message from a delivery driver. He's stuck at the border. You know what our magic is like with vehicles. I sent out a repair crew to make sure he could get here without breaking down again."

There were many benefits to living in a magic community, but if you loved anything electrical, you'd always have problems. "Great. Thanks for doing that. Mom and Granny Dottie have been stressing every day to make sure the celebration is perfect. They spent about a month picking the ideal fairy lights, balloons, and streamers."

"I don't blame them for being stressed. A thousand years of having a demon prison in Willow Tree Falls is something to celebrate. I can't imagine what life would be like if there was nowhere to imprison all those demons."

"And the Crypt witches started it all," Wiggles said. "I'm proud to be a part of the family."

I grinned at him. "Me, too. And once everyone stops stressing over the preparations, we'll have a great time."

As if I'd magicked them to the club, my mom and Granny Dottie marched through the main doors.

"We're here for cocktail ideas." Granny Dottie petted Wiggles and snuck him a meaty chew from out of her huge purse. "Your mom thinks my explosive cocktail mix won't suit all tastes. I don't know what she's talking about. Who doesn't love tequila and magic mixed together?"

I raised a hand.

Granny Dottie tutted at me. "You're a lightweight. What do you suggest we serve at the party?"

"You're the expert when it comes to alcoholic mixes." Mom kissed my cheek and settled on a stool, gratefully accepting a mug of hot chocolate from Merrie.

"Take a look at the menu. I can do anything you like for the party," I said.

They studied the menu for several minutes, pointing out several things they wanted to sample.

"And what about the music?" Granny Dottie said. "Everyone will want a boogie over the demons."

"It's all sorted. The extra drinks are ordered, the decorations are almost here, and the music won't be a problem. Everyone will have a great time," I said.

Mom set down the menu. "I'm sure they will, but it's more than just having fun. We need to remember the Crypt witches who lost their lives defending everyone against the demons. We haven't had a death in the family for years, but we must never forget the fallen."

"We'll have time for the solemn stuff," Granny Dottie said. "I have a list of one hundred and five names I plan to read out."

"You're reading out all those names in the middle of a party?" I said.

"Why not? The least I can do is mention them since they can't be there in person."

"We could do something more discreet. This is a celebration, after all."

"We must respect those who sacrificed their lives so we might live." Granny Dottie thumped me over the head with a cocktail menu.

I ducked and backed away. "Sure. But how about we put up a memorial board? People could drop by and pay their respects and leave offerings to the fallen. Standing there and reading out one hundred and five names of dead witches will kill the mood. It's the opposite of what you want to achieve."

Her lips pursed. "It's not a bad idea. There'll be people coming from other magic communities who knew the deceased. We could ask them to bring photos to put up. How about you—"

"No! Not me. Don't put another thing on my list of party stuff to do," I said. "I still have this place to run and all the party food, drink, and music to finalize."

Mom tweaked the blonde hair out of my bun. "This is cute. When did you do that?"

"Err... maybe this morning. It wasn't there when I got out of bed, though. It must have appeared during the day."

"You changed the color of your hair and didn't realize what you were doing?" Mom's eyes narrowed a fraction.

"Looks like it. Hopefully, it'll fade as quickly as it arrived."

"I like it. Although you should have tried silver. Or green. I once dyed my hair green with yellow tips. Your grandpa said I looked like a beautiful blonde pineapple." Granny Dottie chuckled. "While we're here, let's try some of these cocktails. I've got a thirst on me, and hot chocolate won't quench it."

I grinned at Merrie, who lifted a cocktail maker and shook it. "Sure. We've got a couple of hours before the after-work crowd turns up. What will it be?"

We spent the next hour sampling cocktails, most of them explosively alcoholic under Granny Dottie's orders, and we were all soon laughing and joking and more than a little tipsy.

"We should invite that group of angels to join us." Granny Dottie hiccupped as she slopped her drink on her hand. "They looked tense loitering around outside the front of Angel Force."

I jerked up in my seat, checked the time, and groaned. "No! I'm late."

"For what?" Mom said.

"Dazielle asked me to help. Conan Nox is being brought here to be tried for Violet Oakley's murder."

"Violet Oakley? I know that name." Granny Dottie's forehead wrinkled.

"She was married to Elman." I was already grabbing my jacket and keys.

"The visiting shaman?"

"Yep. And Dazielle needs magical muscle as backup. Conan is a seriously bad guy. He loves using dark magic and curses."

"Oh! I heard about him in the bakery," Granny Dottie said. "What's he doing coming to Willow Tree Falls to be tried for murder?"

I was yanking on my jacket and running to the door. "Don't ask me. I need to go. Wiggles!"

He bounded after me as I ran out the door. "What's the hurry? The angels can handle one guy."

"This is one dark, evil warlock. But I'm not worried about him. Dazielle will be raging because I'm late. And when she gets mad, she gets mean."

"Meaner than usual?"

"Exactly. This won't put me on her good side, and I've got enough to think about without having to dodge an angry angel." I jogged to the brilliant white Angel Force building in the village.

Dazielle stood outside, her foot tapping the ground, her arms crossed, and her wings spread out as far as they'd go. Her brilliant blue gaze latched onto me, and her scowl deepened.

"I know. I'm sorry. I got distracted by Mom and Granny Dottie." I stopped in front of her. "I'm not too late, am I? Conan's not here, is he?"

"You smell like a brewery." Dazielle flipped her long blonde hair over one shoulder and stepped back. "Are you drunk?"

"Mildly tipsy. And it was for research purposes. We were testing cocktails for the party." I grinned at her. Maybe I was tipsier than I realized. "I hope you're coming."

Her scowl didn't improve. "I got my invitation. All the angels did."

"It would be good to see you there." I glanced at the main doors leading into Angel Force. "Granny Dottie saw a group of angels hanging about. Were they waiting for Conan? Am I really too late?"

"Fortunately for you, no. Conan got delayed during processing. He fought an angel, and there were problems with his paperwork. He won't be long."

"So everything is fine." A small hiccup escaped before I could stop it. "Why are you still so grumpy?"

Dazielle jabbed a finger at me. "This is a simple job. Keep an eye on the criminal and make sure he doesn't try anything funny. My angels can be too soft, and you need a firm hand with types like Conan Nox or they'll take advantage."

"You don't need to worry about me being soft on this warlock. After everything I've heard about him, I won't let him out of my sight."

"Make sure you don't until he's in his cell and has nowhere to go. This must go smoothly. Don't let me down."

I splayed my hands. "Have I ever let you down?"

She growled at me. "More times than I care to remember. Let's get inside. Reporters have been hovering, and we don't want them snapping pictures of us looking anxious."

"You're the only one with the anxious face. We're cool as cucumbers."

Wiggles trotted in ahead of us. "And smooth is my middle name."

Dazielle shook her head. "I always thought it was podgy."

Chaos of the Witch is available in paperback and e-book.